GRAPHIC LIBRARY

Qianna and the Quantum Train

# THE GREAT TIME HEIST!

## AN ADVENTURE WITH AN AMERICAN INVENTOR

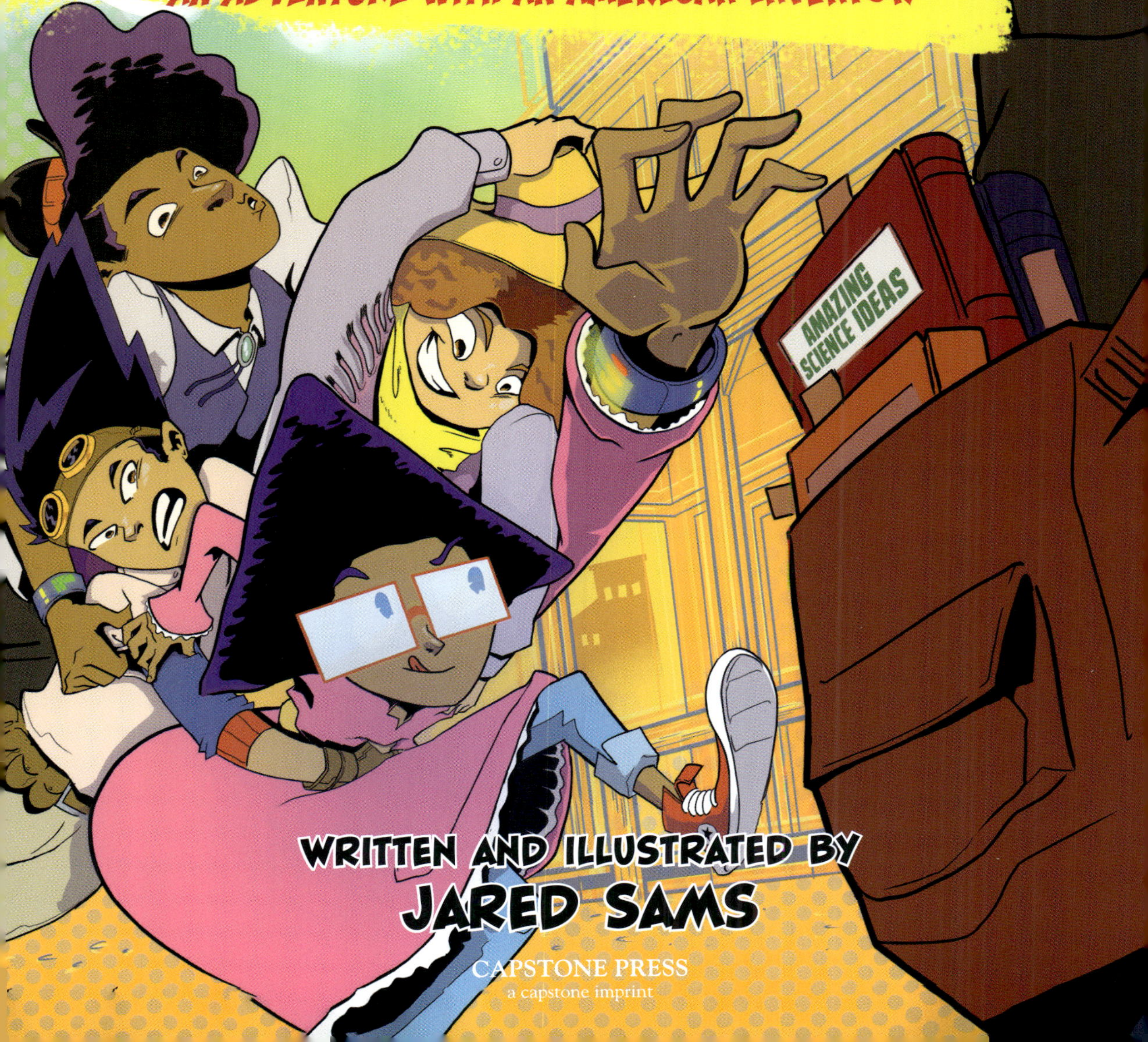
AMAZING SCIENCE IDEAS

WRITTEN AND ILLUSTRATED BY

**JARED SAMS**

CAPSTONE PRESS
a capstone imprint

Published by Capstone Press, an imprint of Capstone
1710 Roe Crest Drive, North Mankato, Minnesota 56003
capstonepub.com

Copyright © 2024 by Capstone. All rights reserved. No part of this publication may be reproduced in whole or in part, or stored in a retrieval system, or transmitted in any form or by any means, electronic, mechanical, photocopying, recording, or otherwise, without written permission of the publisher.

Library of Congress Cataloging-in-Publication Data is is available on the Library of Congress website.
ISBN: 978-1-6690-5569-3 (hardcover)
ISBN: 978-1-6690-5705-5 (paperback)
ISBN: 978-1-6690-5706-2 (ebook PDF)

Summary: Follows Qianna and the Quantum Train crew as they jump back in time to steal a young George Washington Carver's bottomless bag of inventions.

Editorial Credits
Editor: Mari Bolte

Image Credits
Getty Images: Bill Oxford, 28 (bottom left and middle), Corbis/VCG Wilson, 29, Dmitrii Balabanov, 28 (bottom right), Eli Wilson, 28 (top)

Any additional websites and resources referenced in this book are not maintained, authorized, or sponsored by Capstone. All product and company names are trademarks™ or registered® trademarks of their respective holders.

Printed and bound in the USA. 5626

# TABLE OF CONTENTS

**CHAPTER 1:**

The Science Fair Scuffle................... 4

**CHAPTER 2:**

All Aboard the
Quantum Train! ............................... 12

**CHAPTER 3:**

All's Fair at the
Super-Science Fair ....................... 24

> How to File a Patent........................... 28
> Time Tutor Shout-Out! .......................29
> Glossary .............................................. 30
> Read More .......................................... 31
> Internet Sites ......................................31
> About the Author/Illustrator.............32

# CHAPTER 1: THE SCIENCE FAIR SCUFFLE

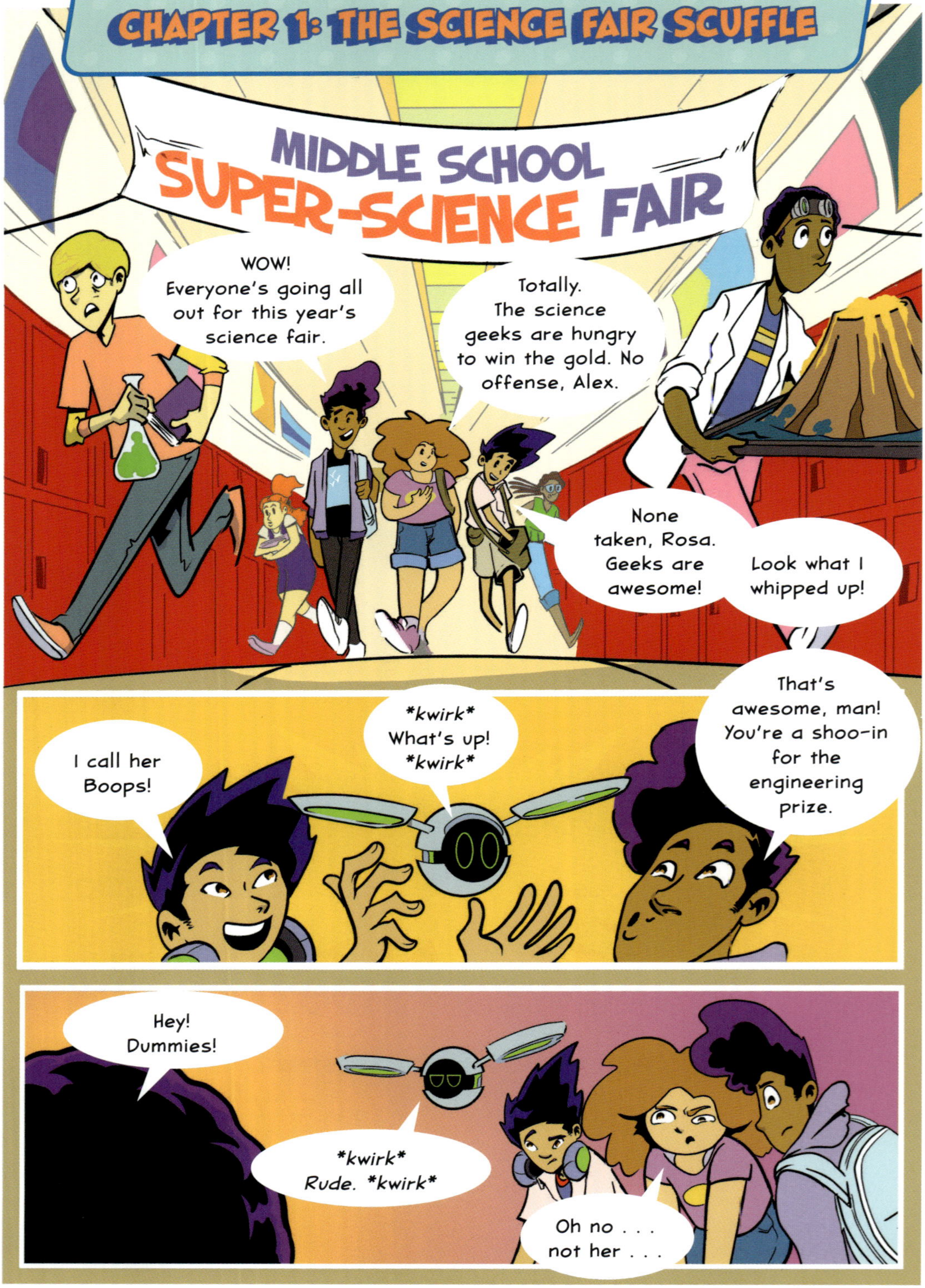
MIDDLE SCHOOL SUPER-SCIENCE FAIR
WOW! Everyone's going all out for this year's science fair.
Totally. The science geeks are hungry to win the gold. No offense, Alex.
None taken, Rosa. Geeks are awesome!
Look what I whipped up!
I call her Boops!
*kwirk* What's up! *kwirk*
That's awesome, man! You're a shoo-in for the engineering prize.
Hey! Dummies!
*kwirk* Rude. *kwirk*
Oh no . . . not her . . .

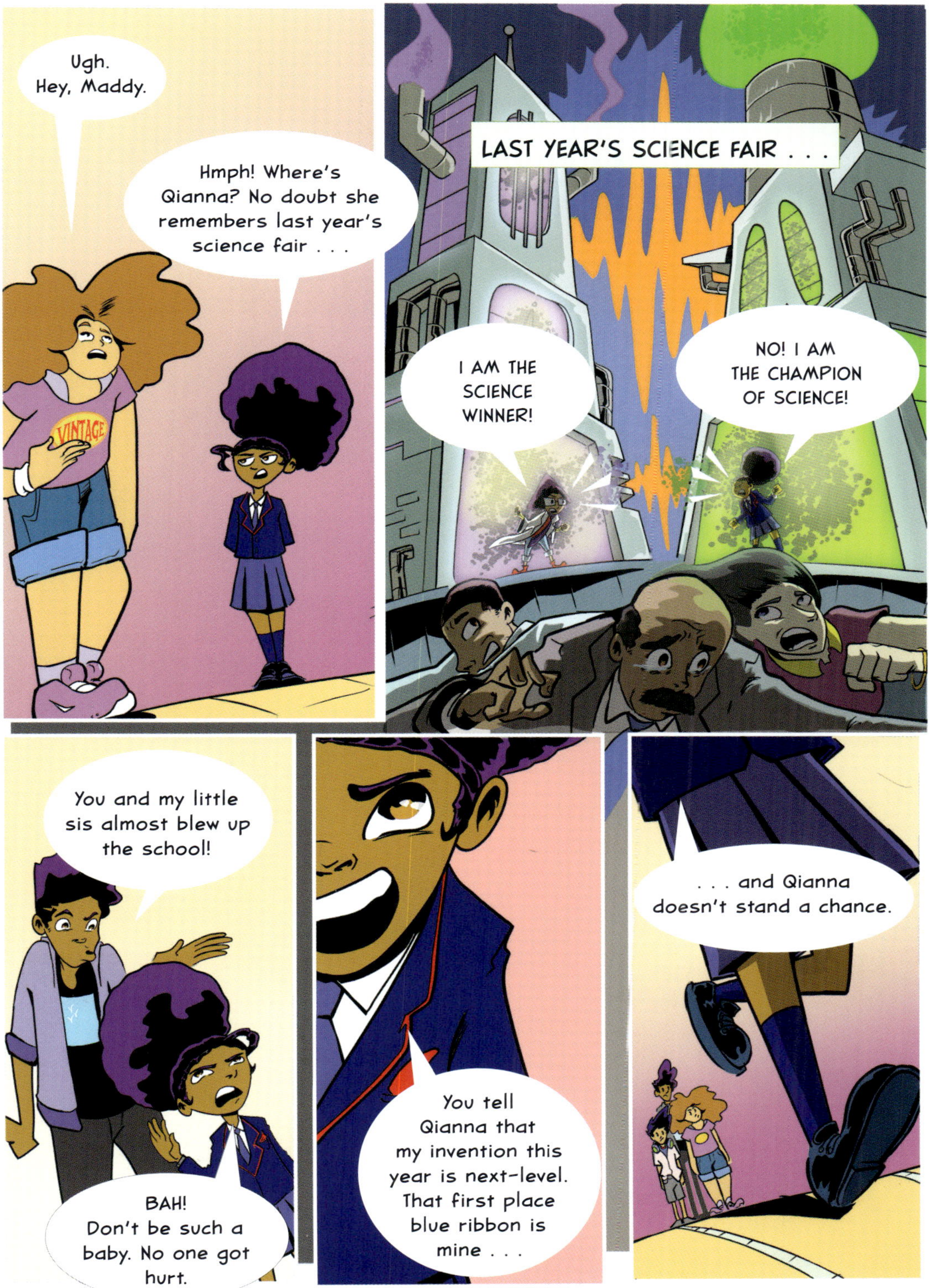
Ugh. Hey, Maddy.
Hmph! Where's Qianna? No doubt she remembers last year's science fair . . .
LAST YEAR'S SCIENCE FAIR . . .
I AM THE SCIENCE WINNER!
NO! I AM THE CHAMPION OF SCIENCE!
You and my little sis almost blew up the school!
BAH! Don't be such a baby. No one got hurt.
You tell Qianna that my invention this year is next-level. That first place blue ribbon is mine . . .
. . . and Qianna doesn't stand a chance.

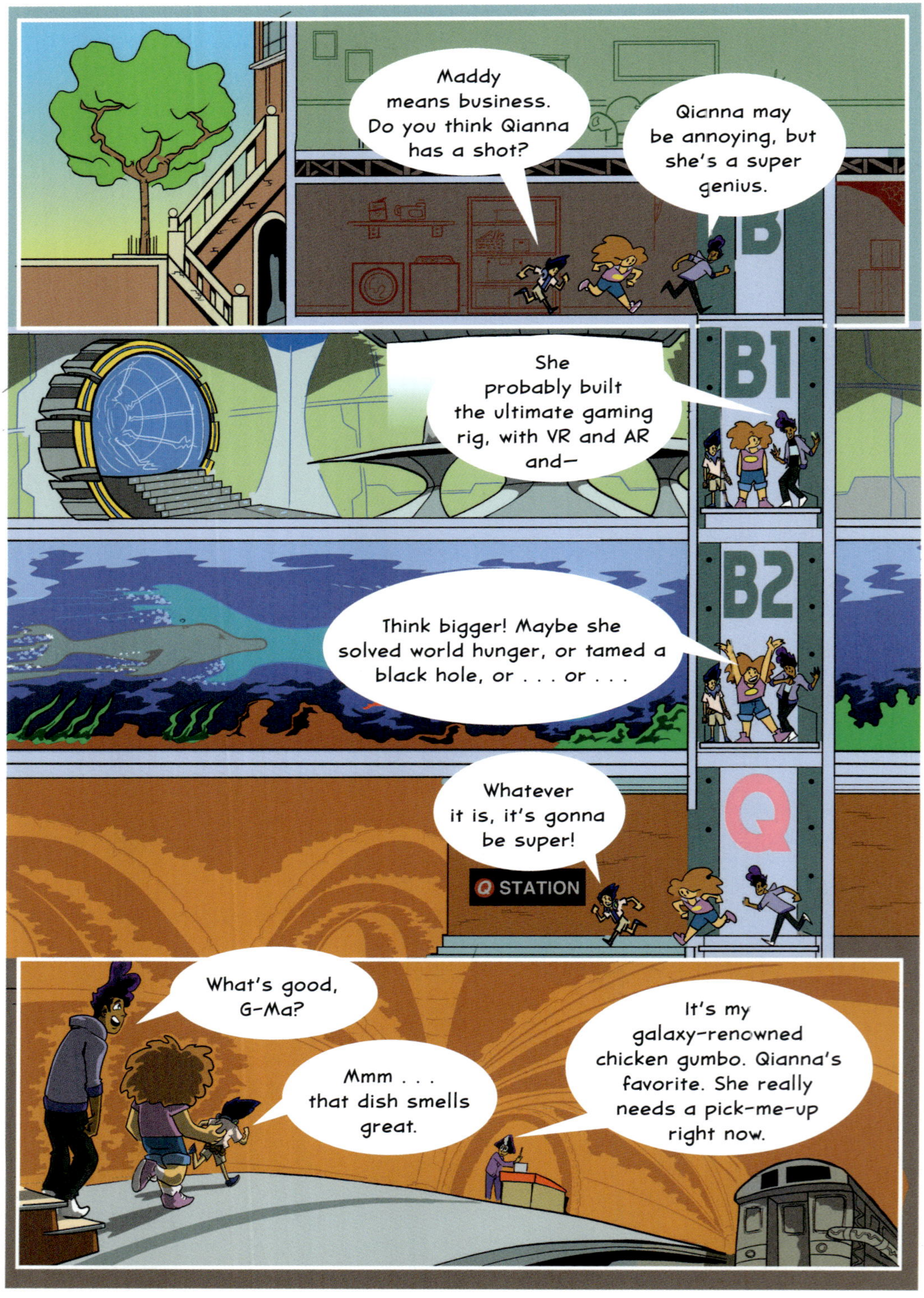

Maddy means business. Do you think Qianna has a shot?
Qianna may be annoying, but she's a super genius.
B
B1
She probably built the ultimate gaming rig, with VR and AR and—
B2
Think bigger! Maybe she solved world hunger, or tamed a black hole, or . . . or . . .
Q
Whatever it is, it's gonna be super!
Q STATION
What's good, G-Ma?
Mmm . . . that dish smells great.
It's my galaxy-renowned chicken gumbo. Qianna's favorite. She really needs a pick-me-up right now.

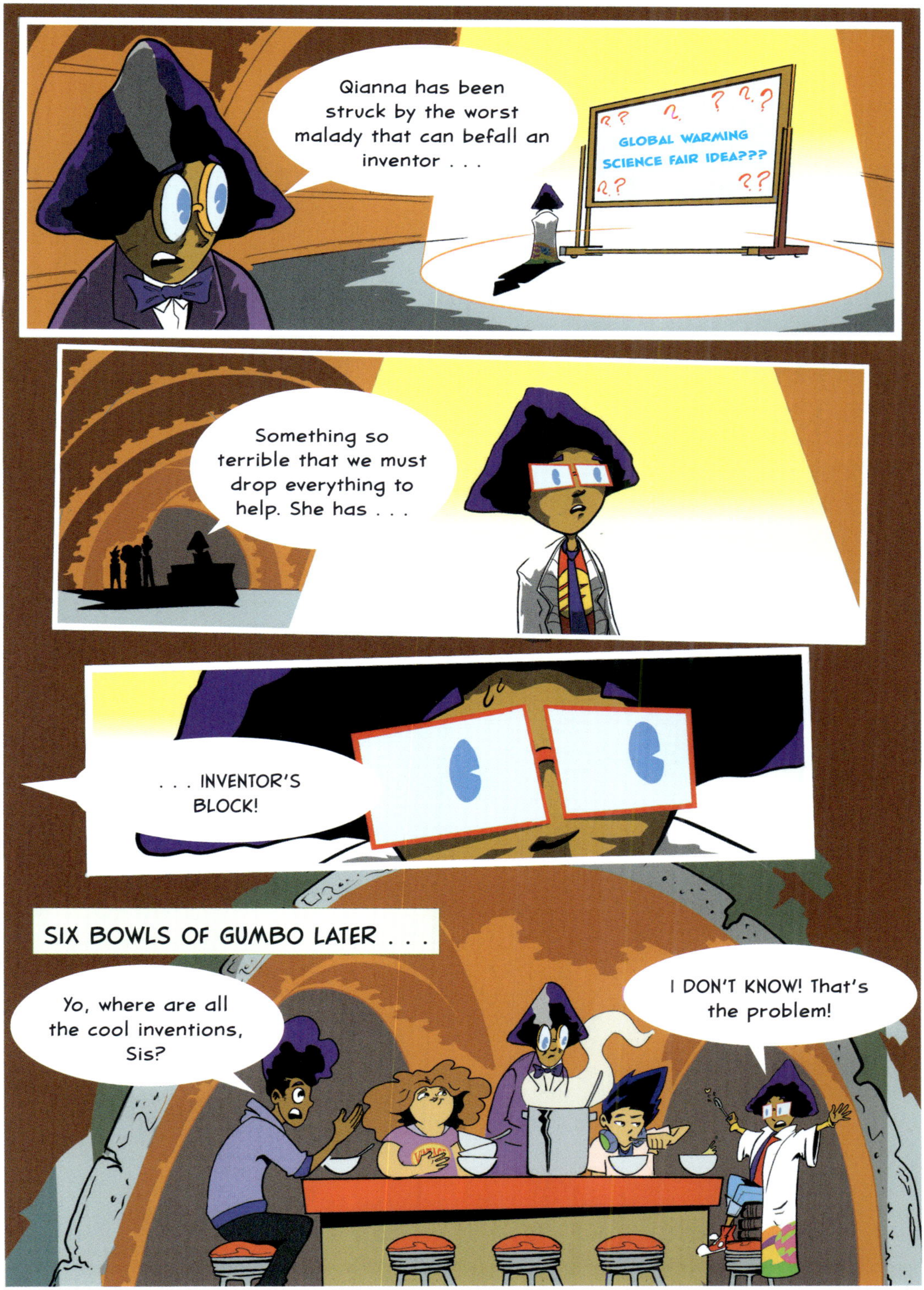

Qianna has been struck by the worst malady that can befall an inventor . . .
GLOBAL WARMING SCIENCE FAIR IDEA???
Something so terrible that we must drop everything to help. She has . . .
. . . INVENTOR'S BLOCK!
SIX BOWLS OF GUMBO LATER . . .
Yo, where are all the cool inventions, Sis?
I DON'T KNOW! That's the problem!

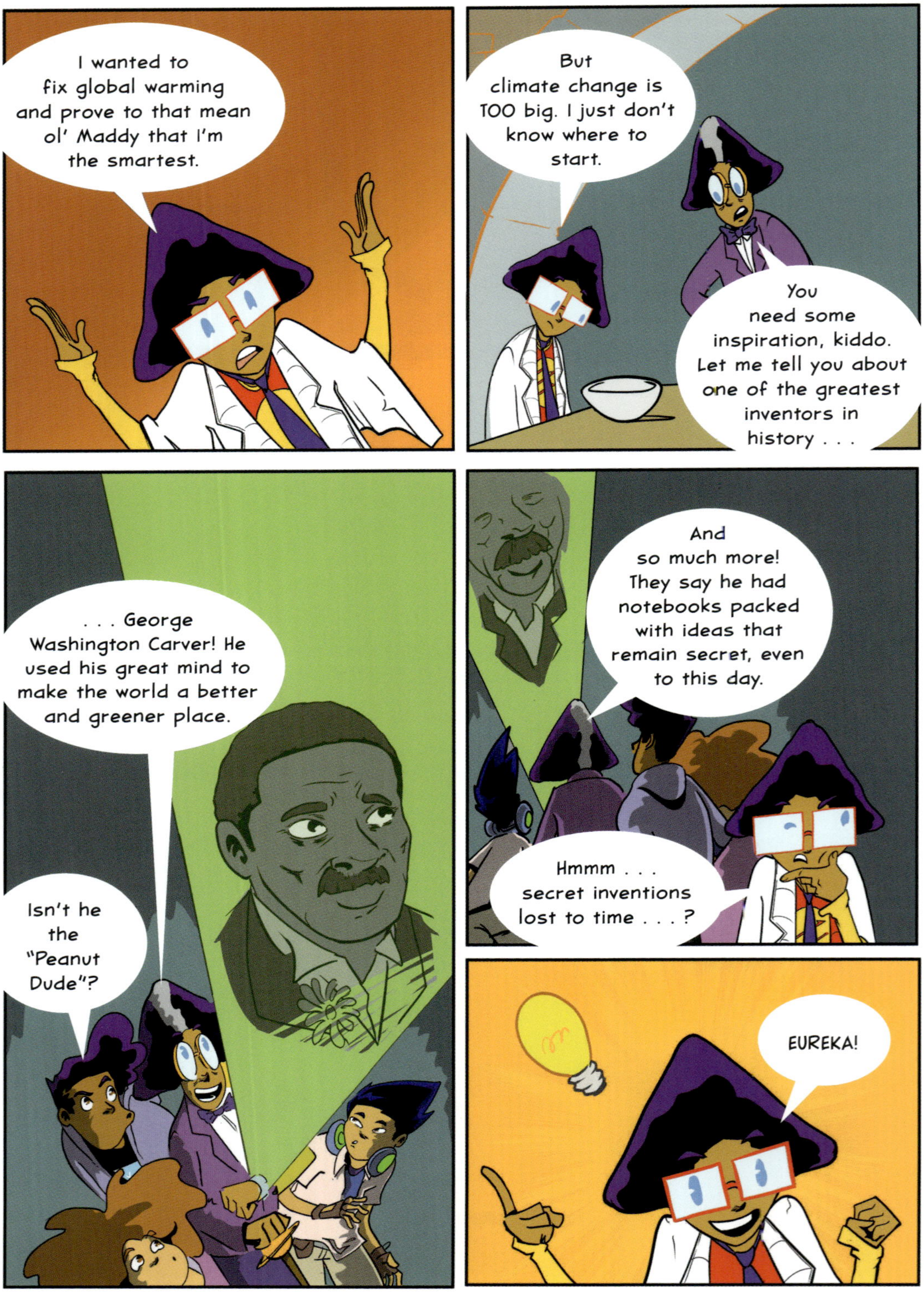
I wanted to fix global warming and prove to that mean ol' Maddy that I'm the smartest.
But climate change is TOO big. I just don't know where to start.
You need some inspiration, kiddo. Let me tell you about one of the greatest inventors in history . . .
. . . George Washington Carver! He used his great mind to make the world a better and greener place.
Isn't he the "Peanut Dude"?
And so much more! They say he had notebooks packed with ideas that remain secret, even to this day.
Hmmm . . . secret inventions lost to time . . . ?
EUREKA!

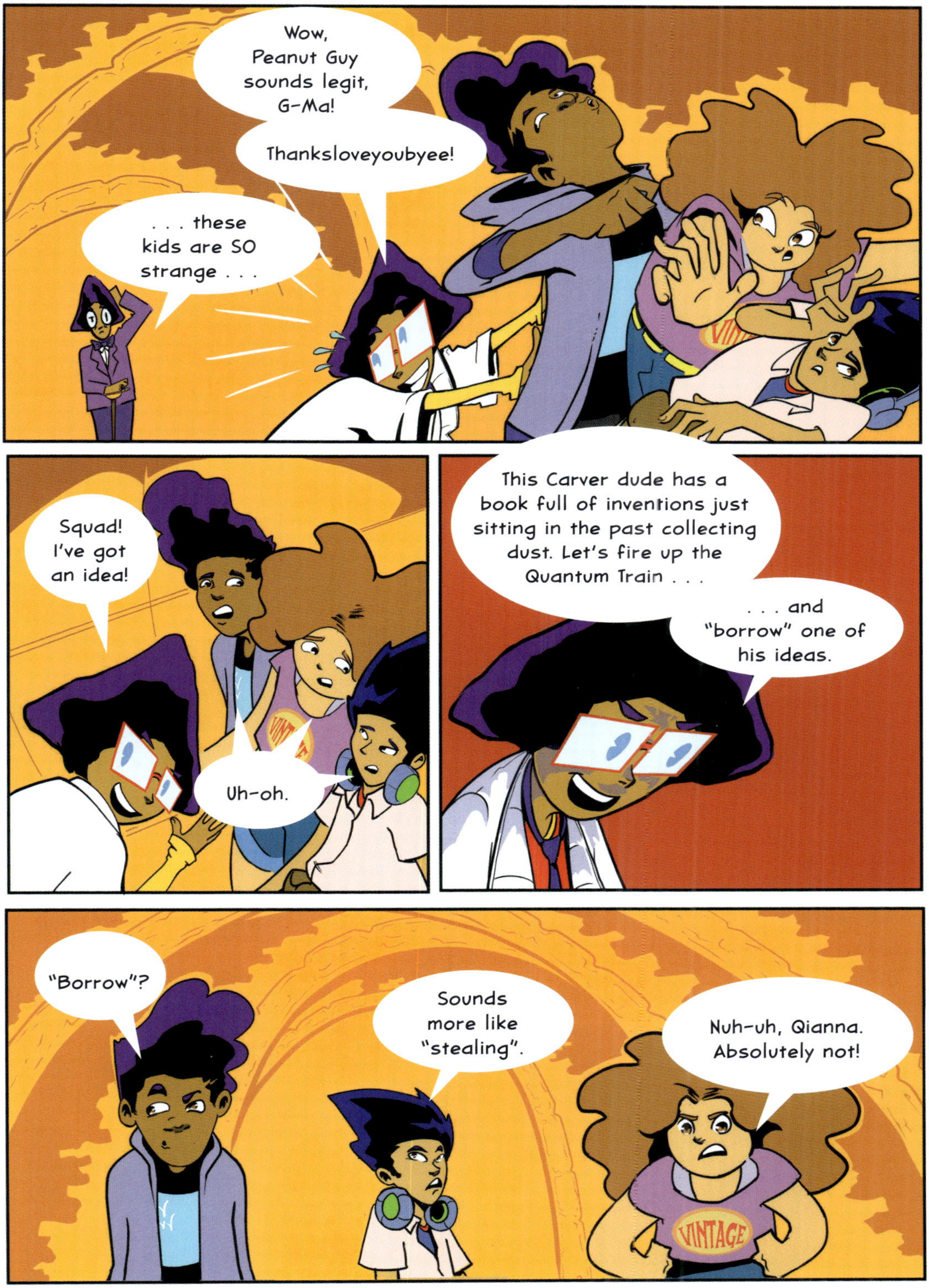
Wow, Peanut Guy sounds legit, G-Ma!
Thanksloveyoubyee!
. . . these kids are SO strange . . .
Squad! I've got an idea!
Uh-oh.
This Carver dude has a book full of inventions just sitting in the past collecting dust. Let's fire up the Quantum Train . . .
. . . and "borrow" one of his ideas.
"Borrow"?
Sounds more like "stealing".
Nuh-uh, Qianna. Absolutely not!

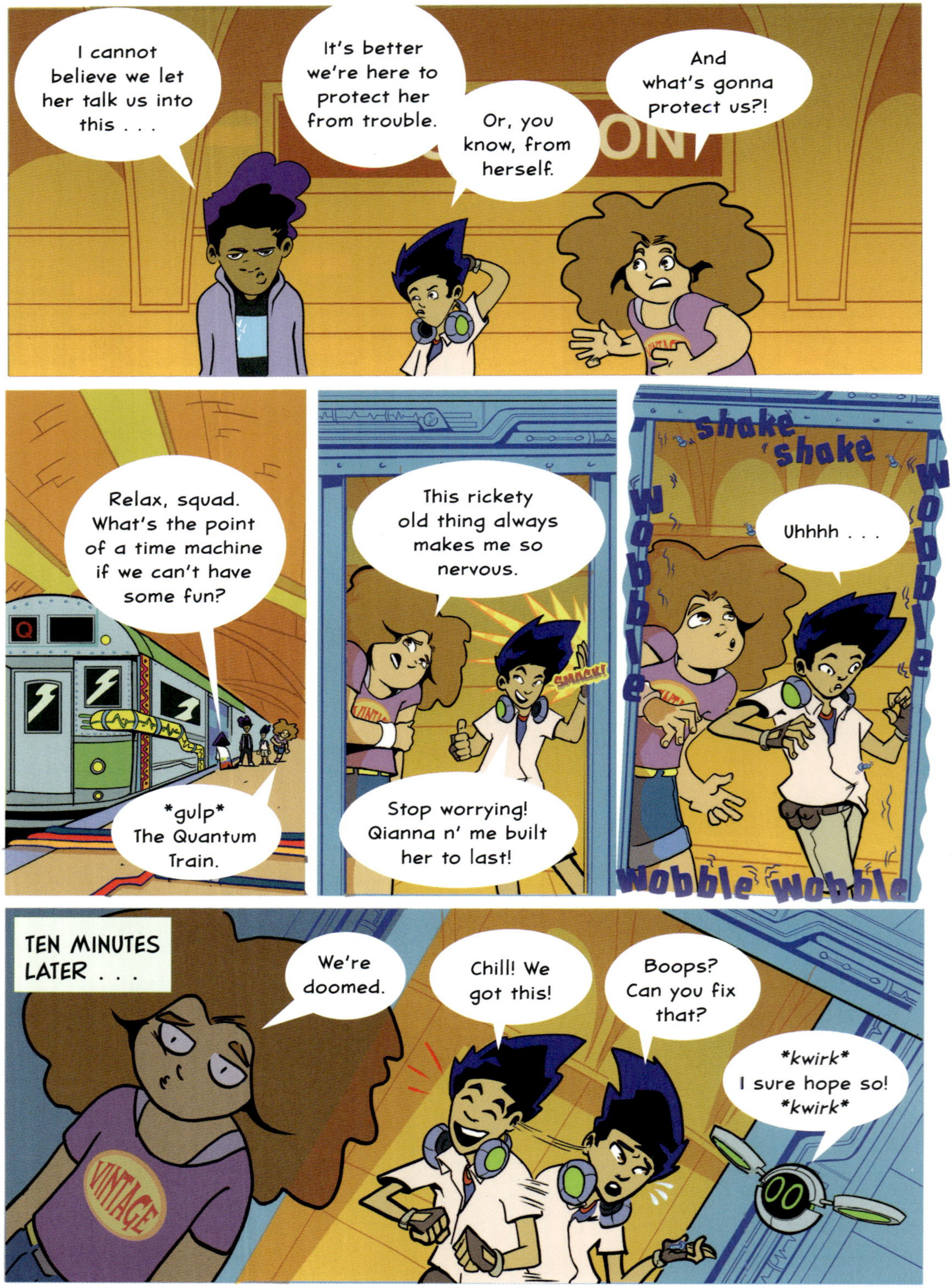
I cannot believe we let her talk us into this . . .
It's better we're here to protect her from trouble.
Or, you know, from herself.
And what's gonna protect us?!
Relax, squad. What's the point of a time machine if we can't have some fun?
*gulp* The Quantum Train.
This rickety old thing always makes me so nervous.
SMACK!
Stop worrying! Qianna n' me built her to last!
shake shake
wobble wobble wobble wobble
Uhhhh . . .
TEN MINUTES LATER . . .
We're doomed.
Chill! We got this!
Boops? Can you fix that?
*kwirk* I sure hope so! *kwirk*

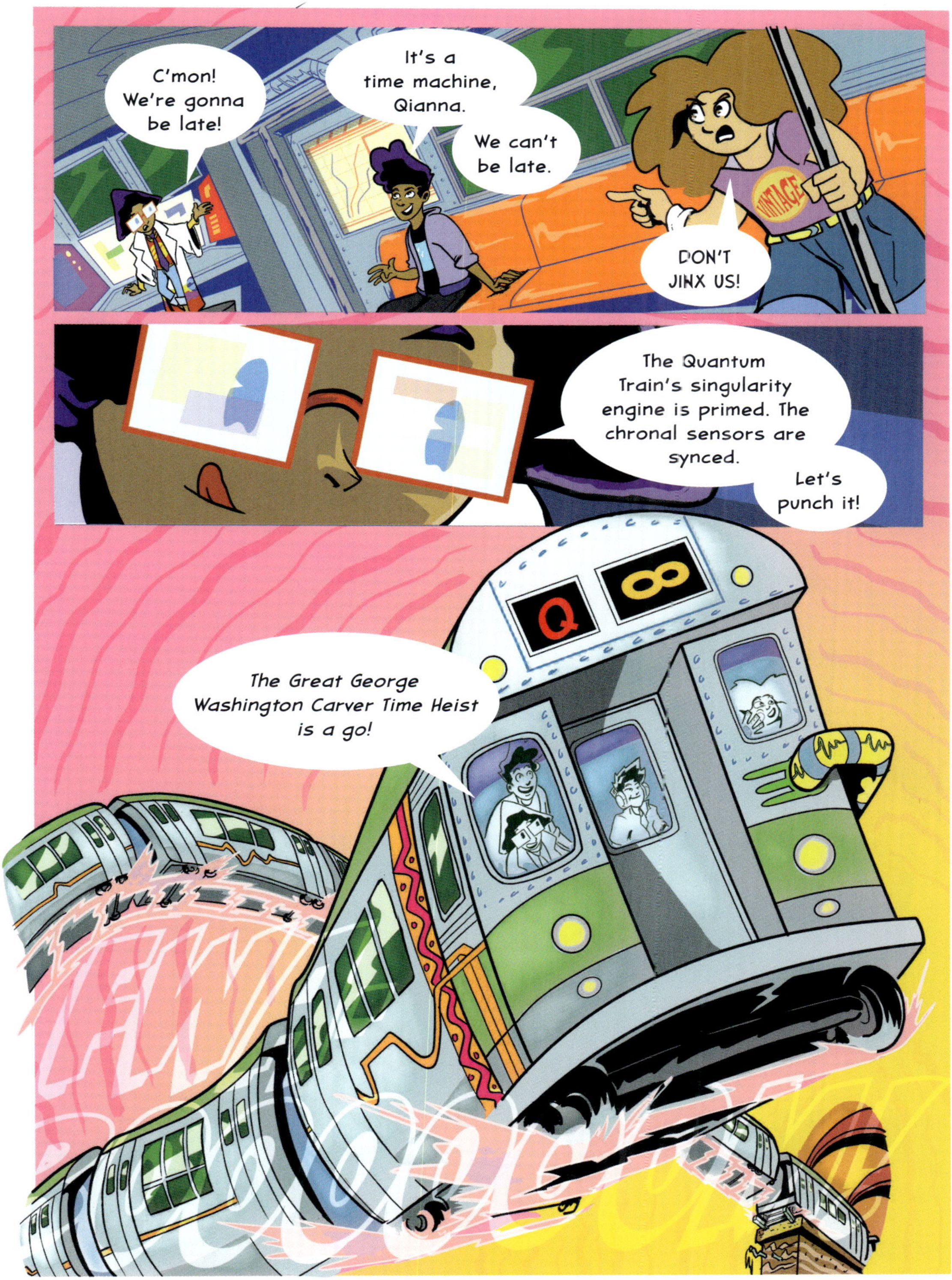
C'mon! We're gonna be late!
It's a time machine, Qianna.
We can't be late.
DON'T JINX US!
The Quantum Train's singularity engine is primed. The chronal sensors are synced.
Let's punch it!
The Great George Washington Carver Time Heist is a go!
Q
∞
VINTAGE

# CHAPTER 2: ALL ABOARD THE QUANTUM TRAIN!

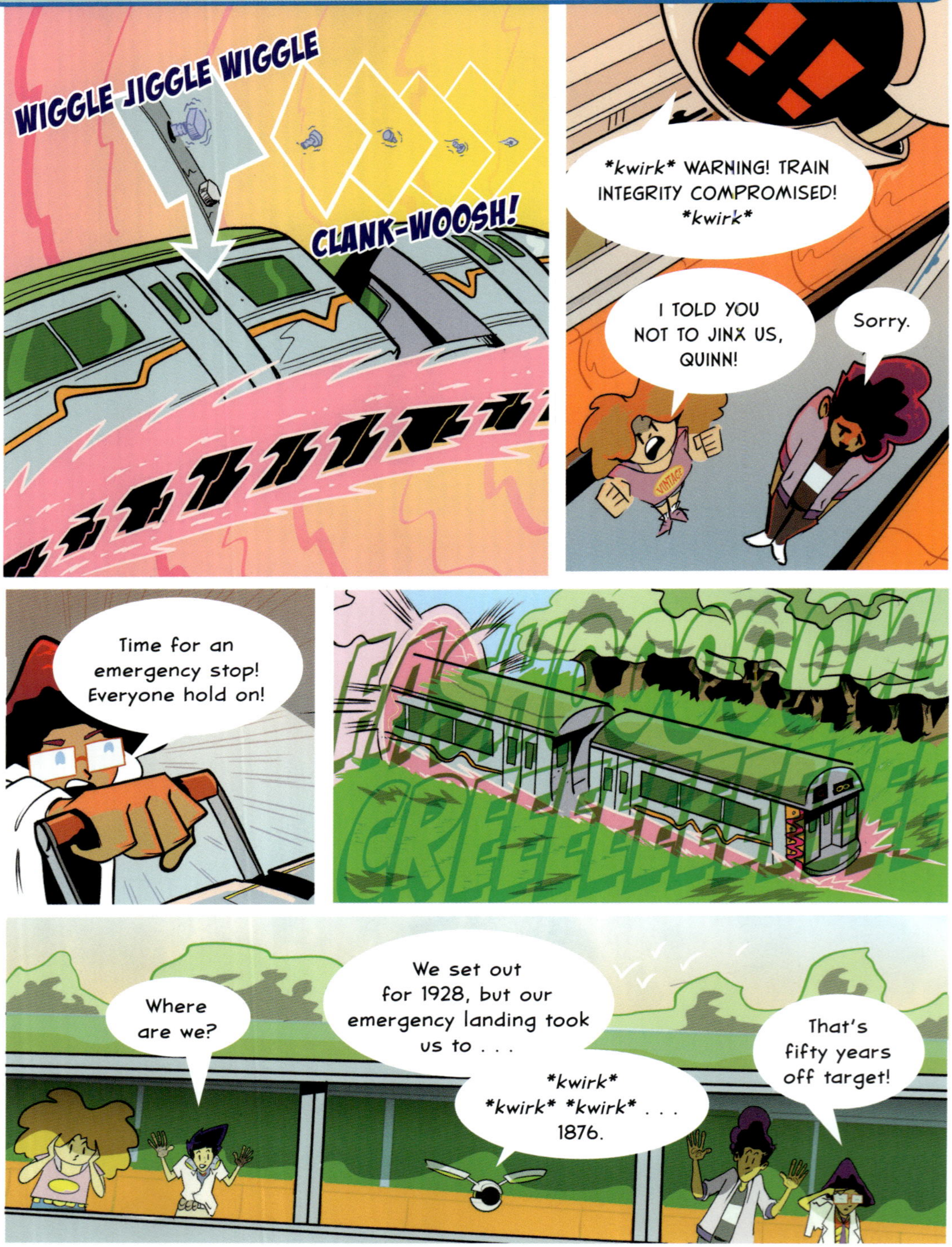
WIGGLE JIGGLE WIGGLE
CLANK-WOOSH!
*kwirk* WARNING! TRAIN INTEGRITY COMPROMISED! *kwirk*
I TOLD YOU NOT TO JINX US, QUINN!
Sorry.
VINTAGE
Time for an emergency stop! Everyone hold on!
Where are we?
We set out for 1928, but our emergency landing took us to . . .
*kwirk* *kwirk* *kwirk* . . . 1876.
That's fifty years off target!

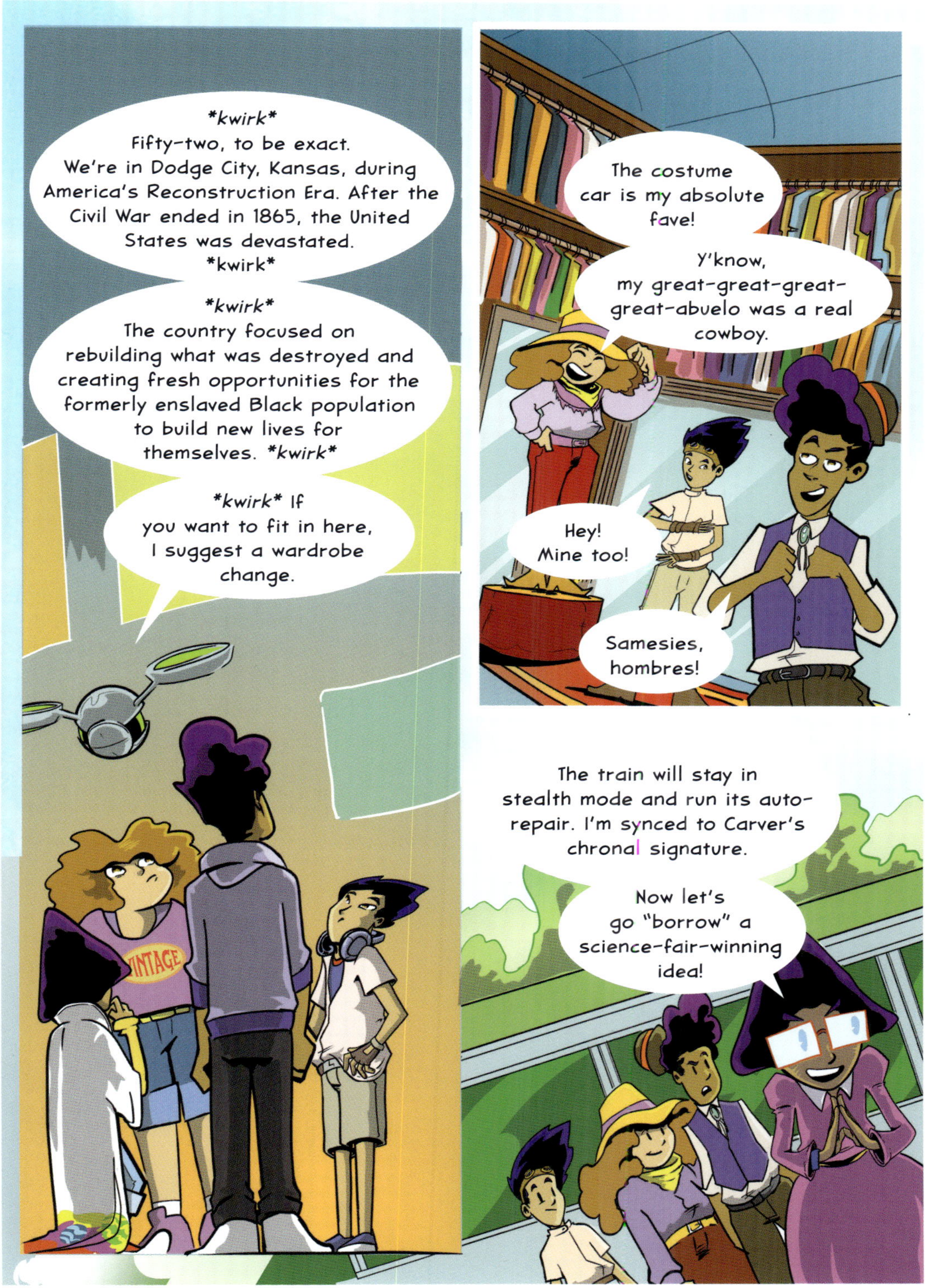
*kwirk*
Fifty-two, to be exact.
We're in Dodge City, Kansas, during America's Reconstruction Era. After the Civil War ended in 1865, the United States was devastated. *kwirk*
*kwirk*
The country focused on rebuilding what was destroyed and creating fresh opportunities for the formerly enslaved Black population to build new lives for themselves. *kwirk*
*kwirk* If you want to fit in here, I suggest a wardrobe change.
VINTAGE
The costume car is my absolute fave!
Y'know, my great-great-great-great-abuelo was a real cowboy.
Hey! Mine too!
Samesies, hombres!
The train will stay in stealth mode and run its auto-repair. I'm synced to Carver's chronal signature.
Now let's go "borrow" a science-fair-winning idea!

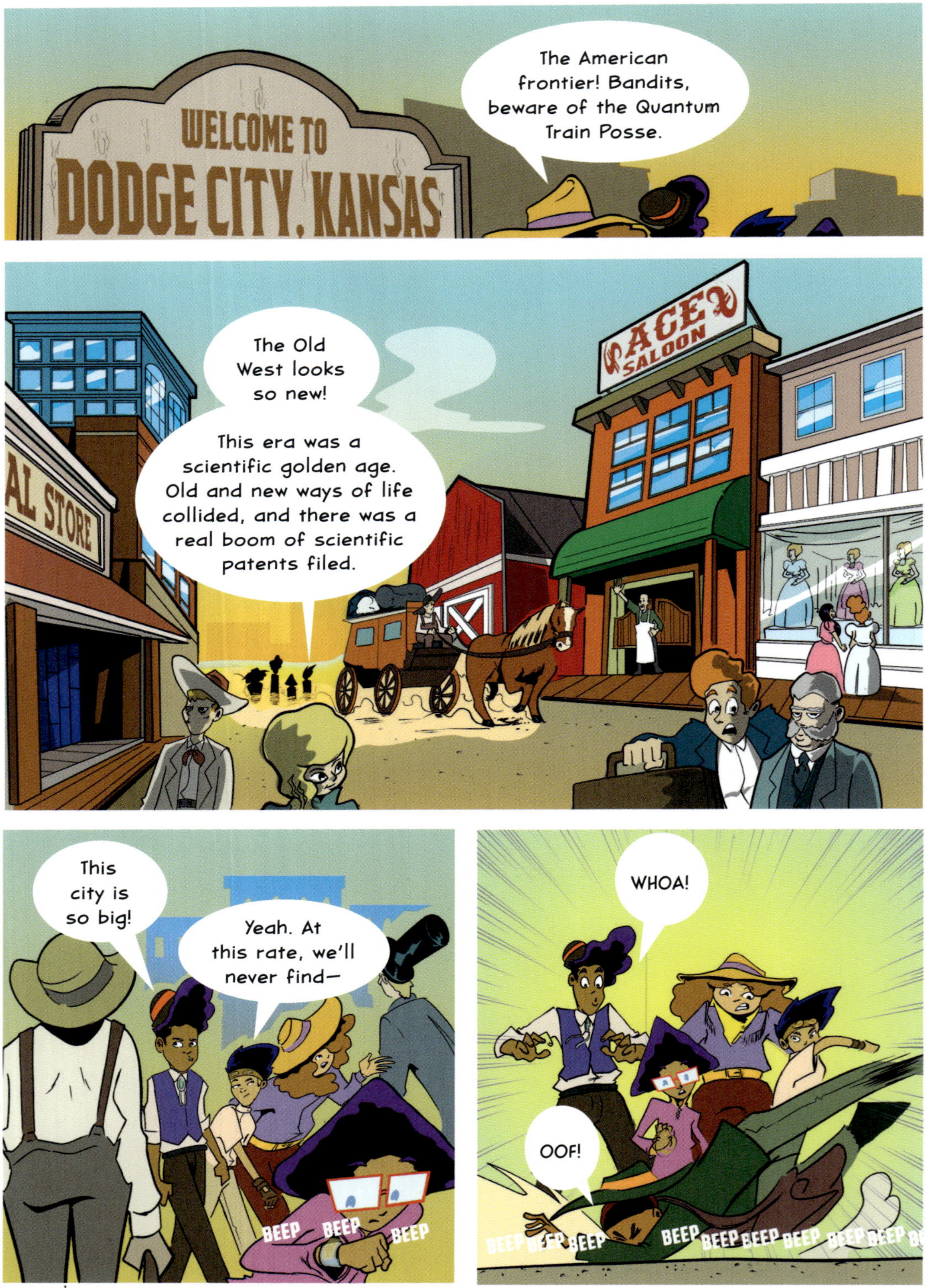
WELCOME TO
DODGE CITY, KANSAS
The American frontier! Bandits, beware of the Quantum Train Posse.
ACE SALOON
AL STORE
The Old West looks so new!
This era was a scientific golden age. Old and new ways of life collided, and there was a real boom of scientific patents filed.
This city is so big!
Yeah. At this rate, we'll never find—
BEEP BEEP BEEP
WHOA!
OOF!
BEEP BEEP BEEP BEEP BEEP BEEP BEEP BEEP BEEP

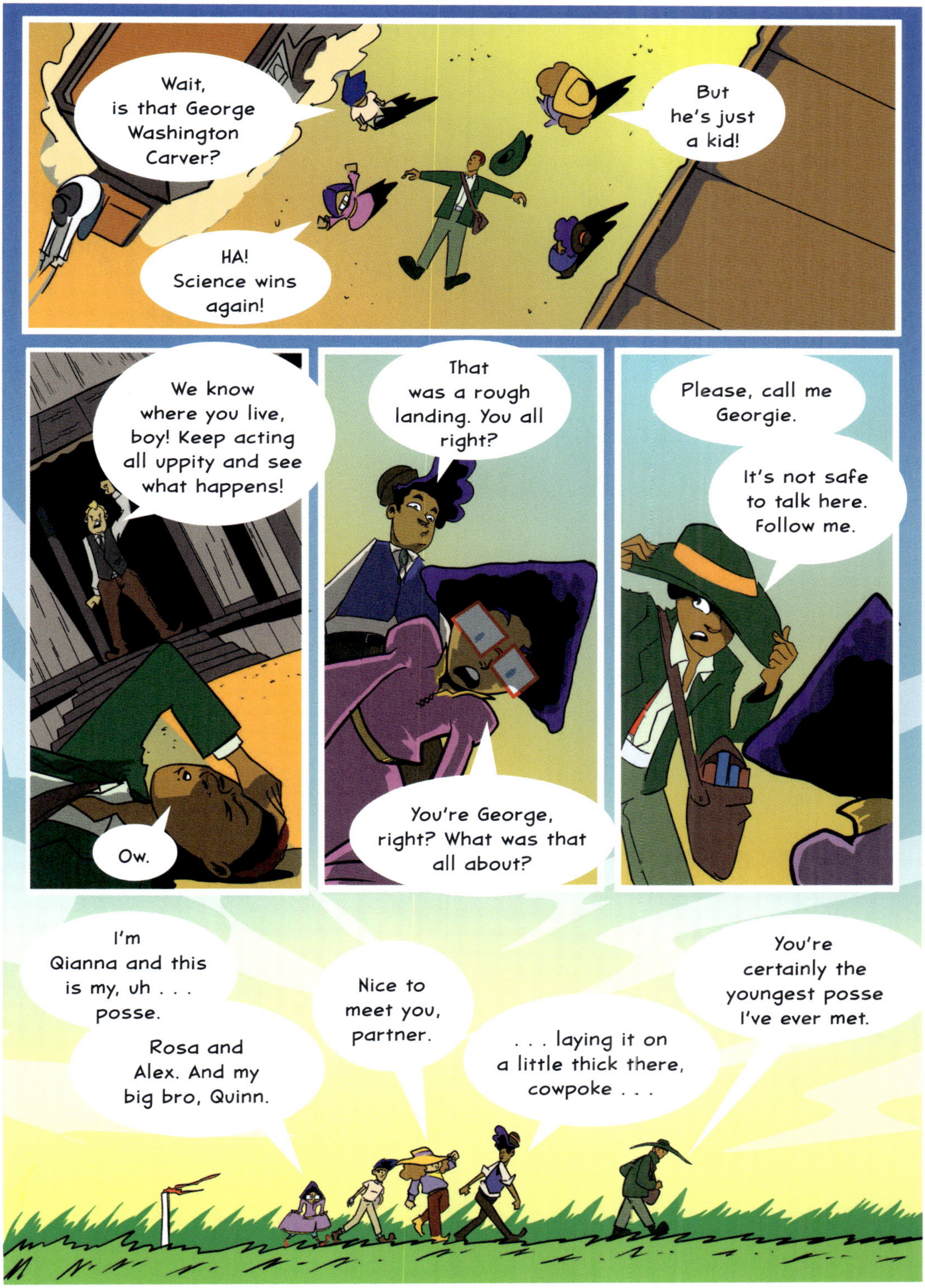
Wait, is that George Washington Carver?
But he's just a kid!
HA! Science wins again!
We know where you live, boy! Keep acting all uppity and see what happens!
Ow.
That was a rough landing. You all right?
You're George, right? What was that all about?
Please, call me Georgie.
It's not safe to talk here. Follow me.
I'm Qianna and this is my, uh . . . posse.
Rosa and Alex. And my big bro, Quinn.
Nice to meet you, partner.
. . . laying it on a little thick there, cowpoke . . .
You're certainly the youngest posse I've ever met.

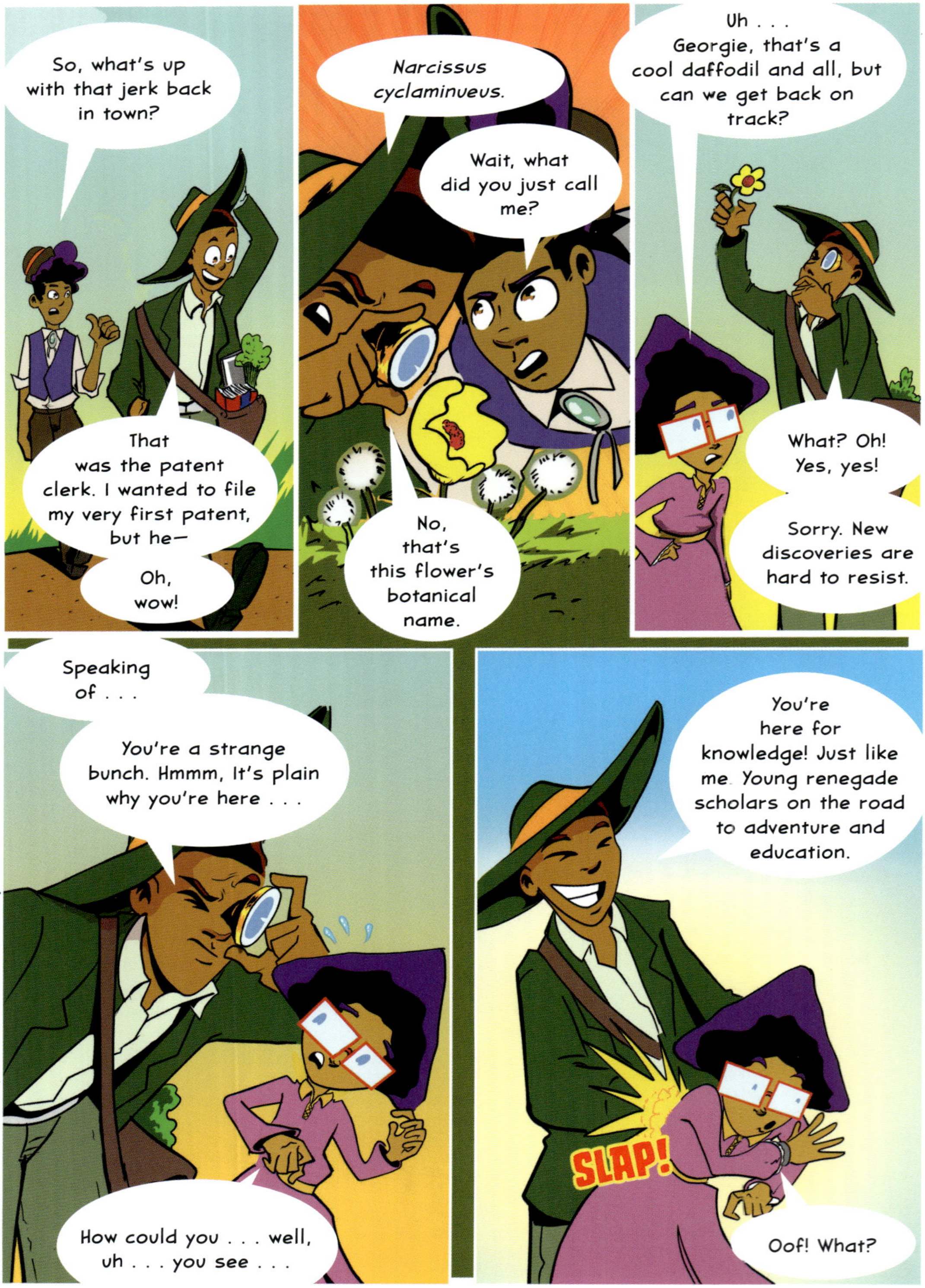

So, what's up with that jerk back in town?
That was the patent clerk. I wanted to file my very first patent, but he—
Oh, wow!
Narcissus cyclaminueus.
Wait, what did you just call me?
No, that's this flower's botanical name.
Uh . . . Georgie, that's a cool daffodil and all, but can we get back on track?
What? Oh! Yes, yes!
Sorry. New discoveries are hard to resist.
Speaking of . . .
You're a strange bunch. Hmmm, It's plain why you're here . . .
How could you . . . well, uh . . . you see . . .
You're here for knowledge! Just like me. Young renegade scholars on the road to adventure and education.
SLAP!
Oof! What?

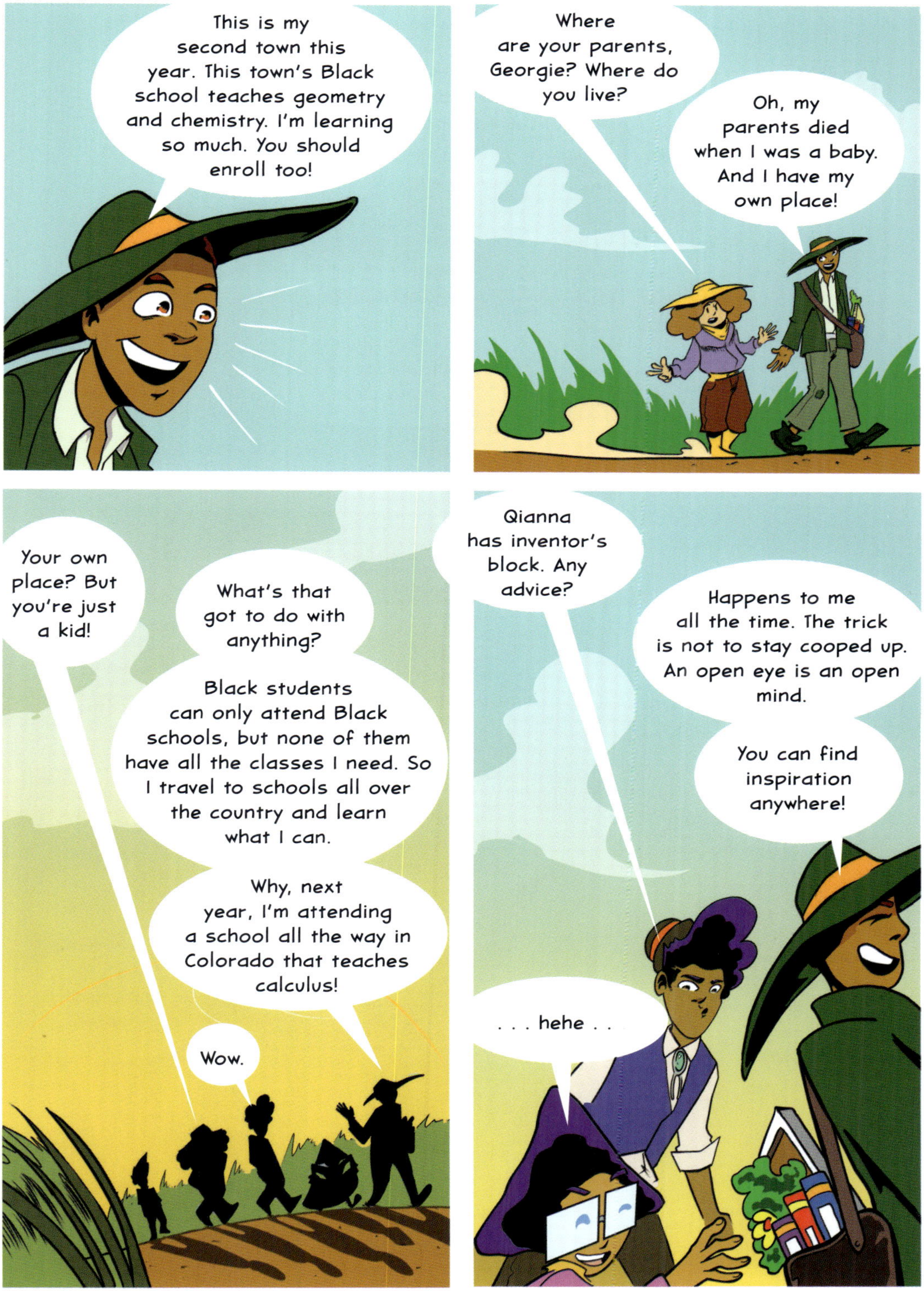
This is my second town this year. This town's Black school teaches geometry and chemistry. I'm learning so much. You should enroll too!
Where are your parents, Georgie? Where do you live?
Oh, my parents died when I was a baby. And I have my own place!
Your own place? But you're just a kid!
What's that got to do with anything?
Black students can only attend Black schools, but none of them have all the classes I need. So I travel to schools all over the country and learn what I can.
Why, next year, I'm attending a school all the way in Colorado that teaches calculus!
Wow.
Qianna has inventor's block. Any advice?
Happens to me all the time. The trick is not to stay cooped up. An open eye is an open mind.
You can find inspiration anywhere!
. . . hehe . .

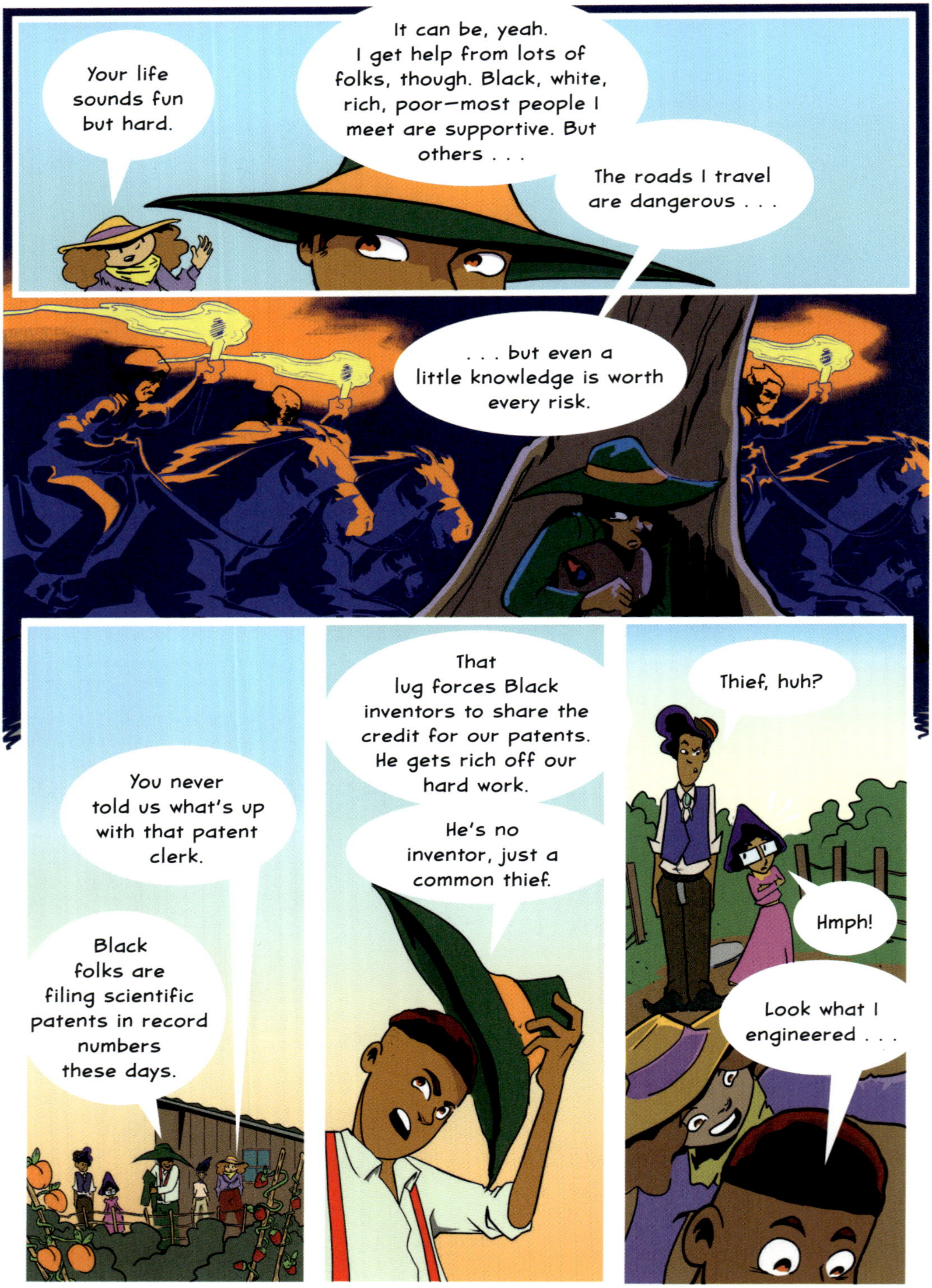
Your life sounds fun but hard.
It can be, yeah. I get help from lots of folks, though. Black, white, rich, poor—most people I meet are supportive. But others . . .
The roads I travel are dangerous . . .
. . . but even a little knowledge is worth every risk.
You never told us what's up with that patent clerk.
Black folks are filing scientific patents in record numbers these days.
That lug forces Black inventors to share the credit for our patents. He gets rich off our hard work.
He's no inventor, just a common thief.
Thief, huh?
Hmph!
Look what I engineered . . .

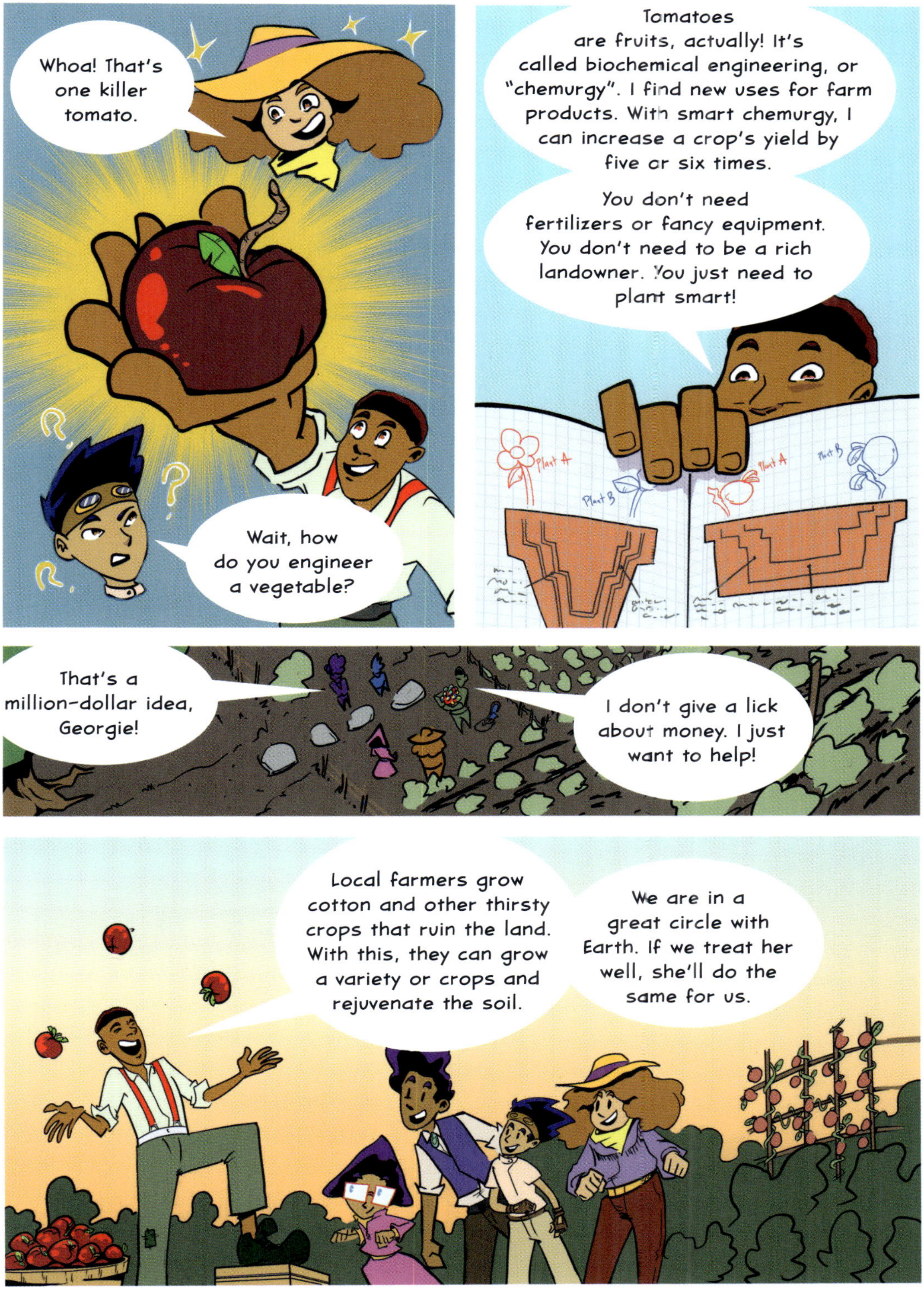
Whoa! That's one killer tomato.
Wait, how do you engineer a vegetable?
Tomatoes are fruits, actually! It's called biochemical engineering, or "chemurgy". I find new uses for farm products. With smart chemurgy, I can increase a crop's yield by five or six times.
You don't need fertilizers or fancy equipment. You don't need to be a rich landowner. You just need to plant smart!
Plant A
Plant B
Plant A
Plant B
That's a million-dollar idea, Georgie!
I don't give a lick about money. I just want to help!
Local farmers grow cotton and other thirsty crops that ruin the land. With this, they can grow a variety or crops and rejuvenate the soil.
We are in a great circle with Earth. If we treat her well, she'll do the same for us.

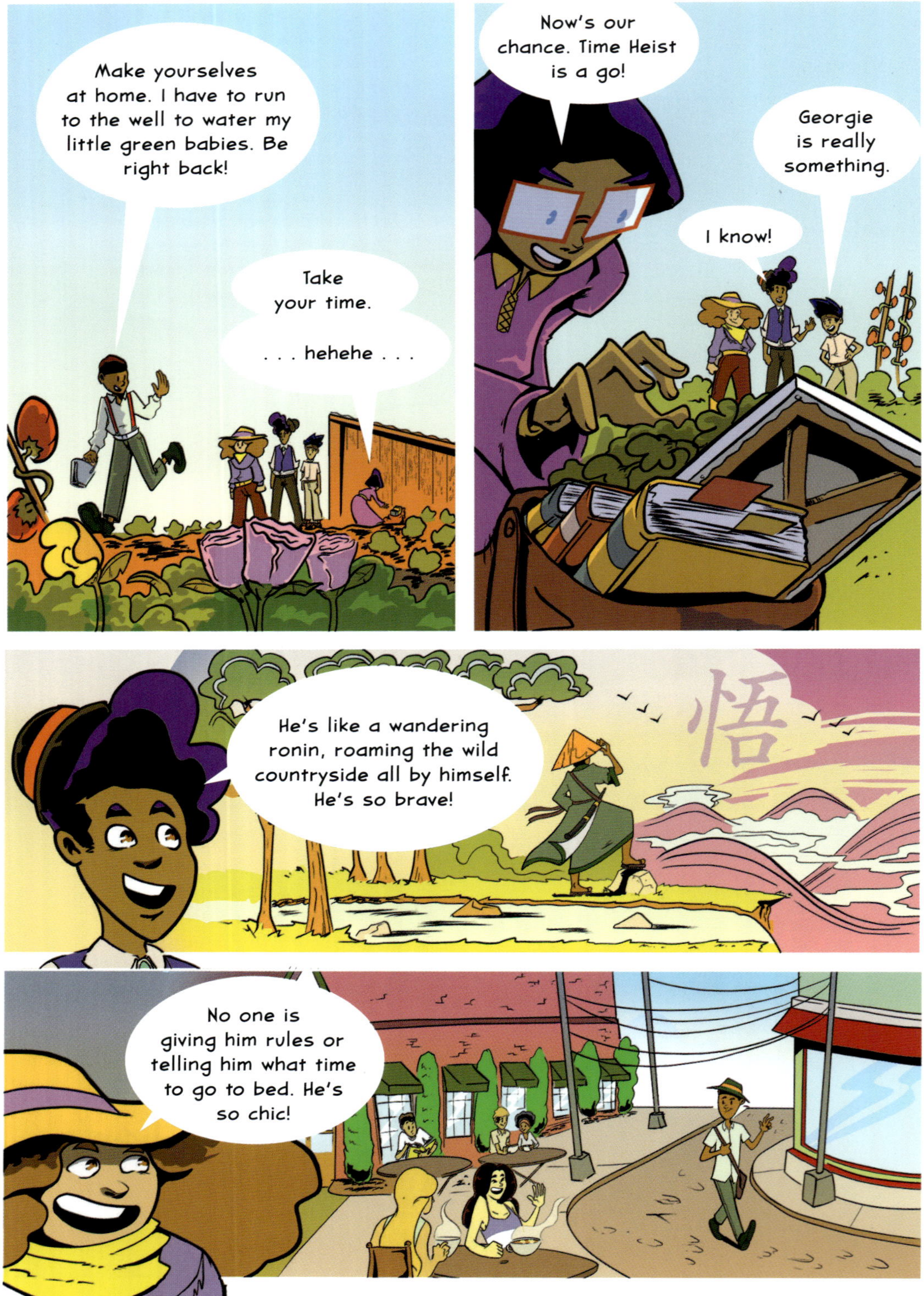
Make yourselves at home. I have to run to the well to water my little green babies. Be right back!
Take your time.
. . . hehehe . . .
Now's our chance. Time Heist is a go!
Georgie is really something.
I know!
He's like a wandering ronin, roaming the wild countryside all by himself. He's so brave!
悟
No one is giving him rules or telling him what time to go to bed. He's so chic!

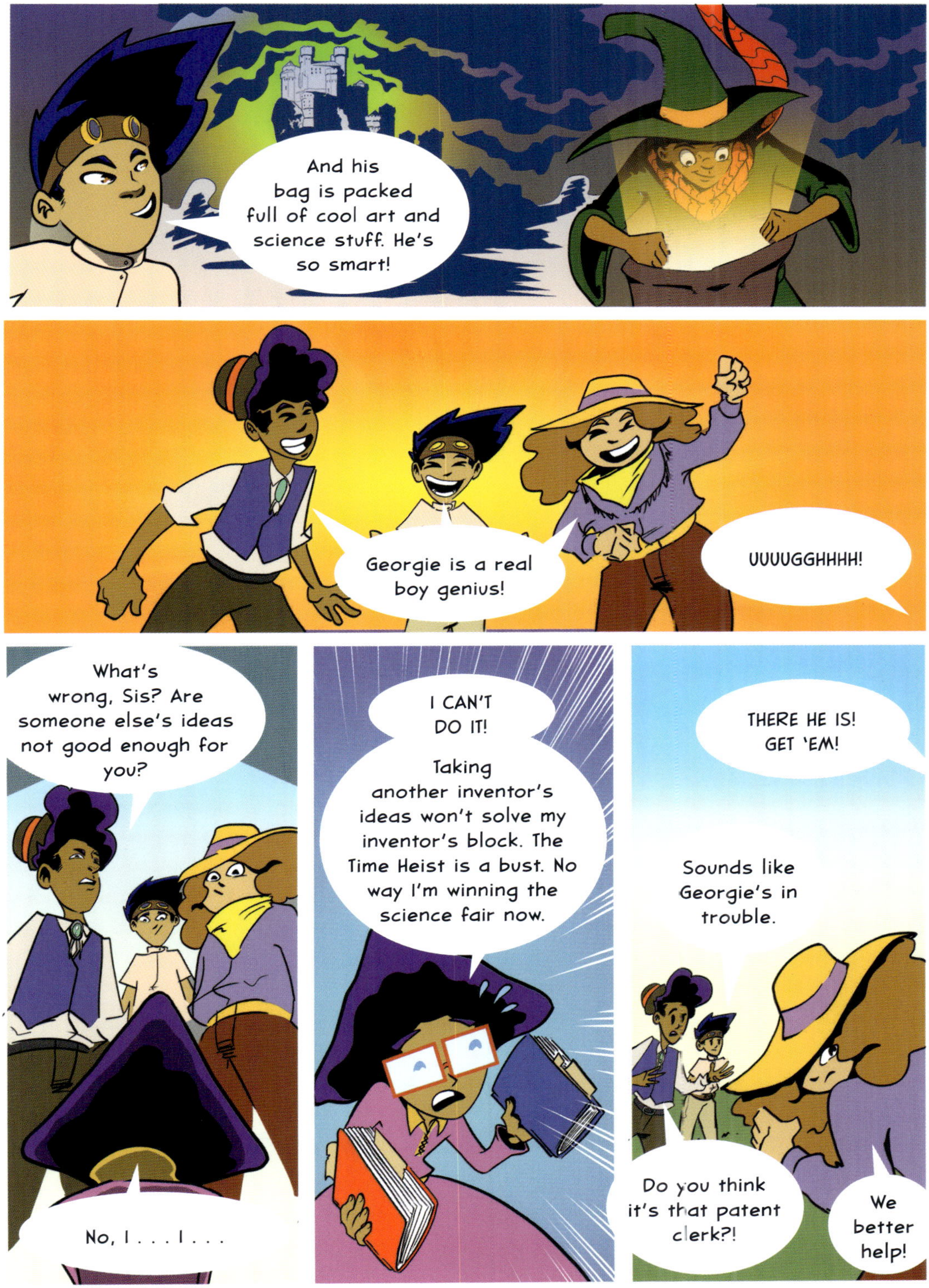
And his bag is packed full of cool art and science stuff. He's so smart!
Georgie is a real boy genius!
UUUUGGHHHH!
What's wrong, Sis? Are someone else's ideas not good enough for you?
No, I . . . I . . .
I CAN'T DO IT!
Taking another inventor's ideas won't solve my inventor's block. The Time Heist is a bust. No way I'm winning the science fair now.
THERE HE IS! GET 'EM!
Sounds like Georgie's in trouble.
Do you think it's that patent clerk?!
We better help!

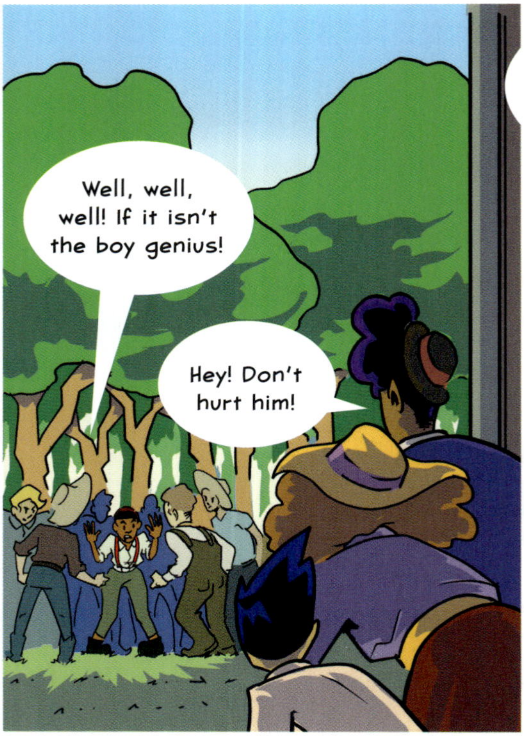
Well, well, well! If it isn't the boy genius!
Hey! Don't hurt him!

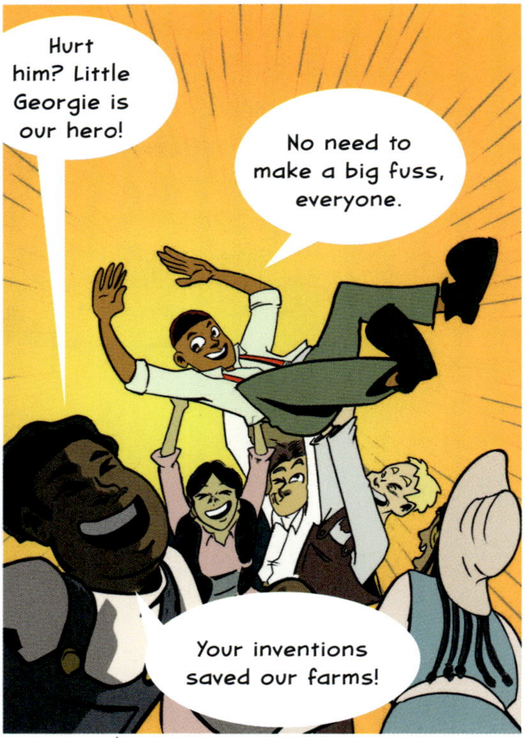
Hurt him? Little Georgie is our hero!
No need to make a big fuss, everyone.
Your inventions saved our farms!

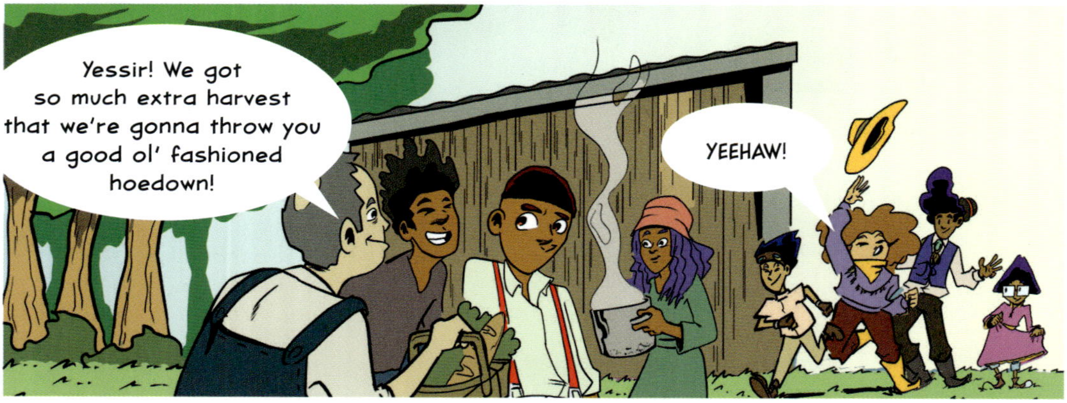
Yessir! We got so much extra harvest that we're gonna throw you a good ol' fashioned hoedown!
YEEHAW!

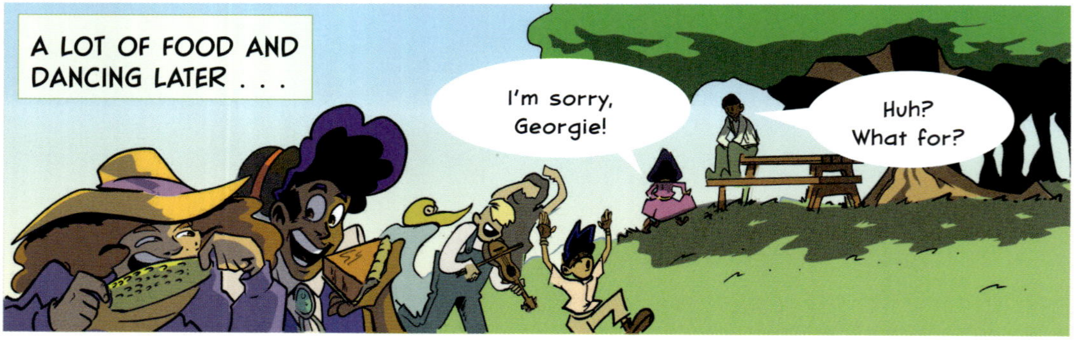
A LOT OF FOOD AND DANCING LATER . . .
I'm sorry, Georgie!
Huh? What for?

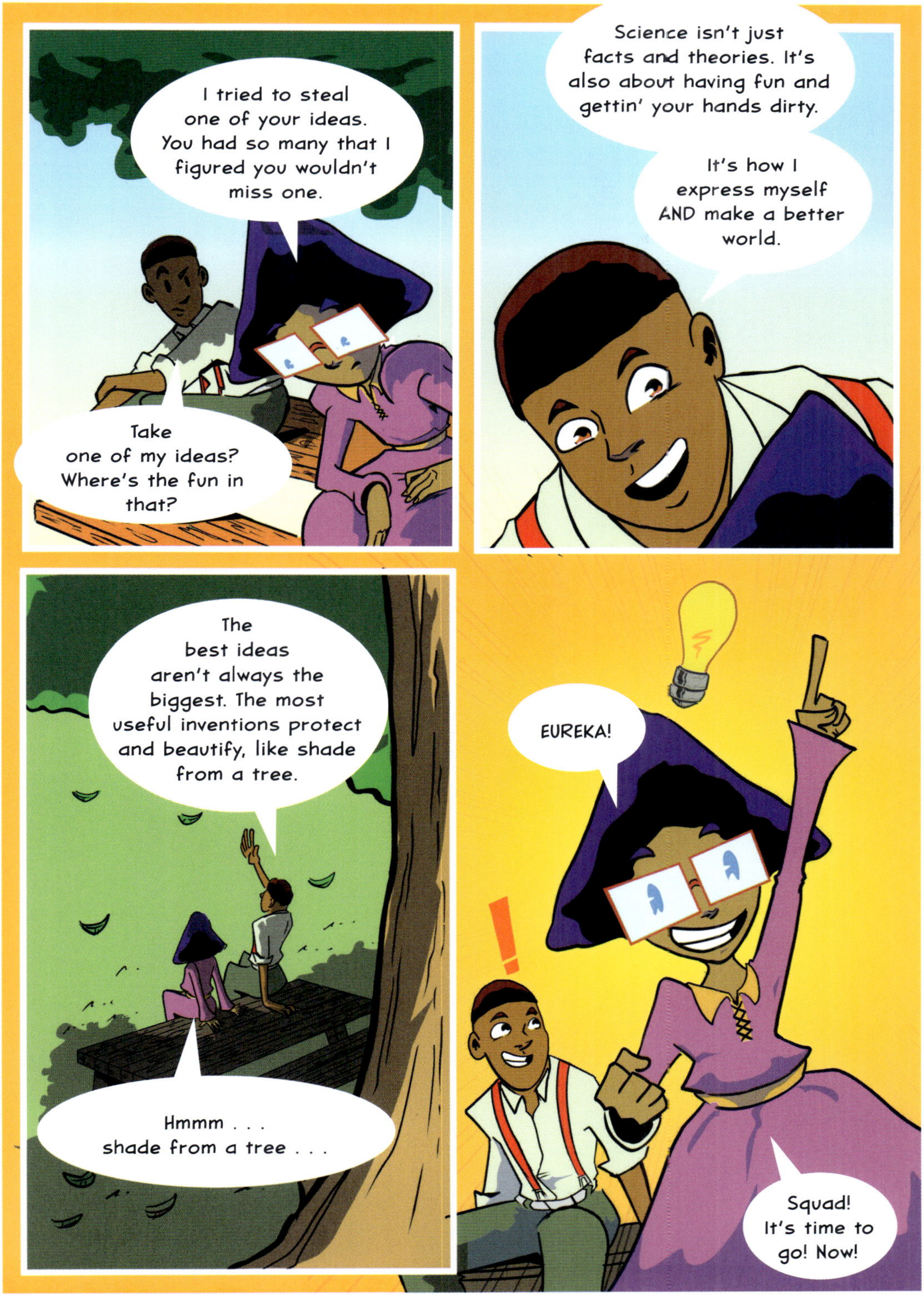
I tried to steal one of your ideas. You had so many that I figured you wouldn't miss one.
Take one of my ideas? Where's the fun in that?
Science isn't just facts and theories. It's also about having fun and gettin' your hands dirty.
It's how I express myself AND make a better world.
The best ideas aren't always the biggest. The most useful inventions protect and beautify, like shade from a tree.
Hmmm . . . shade from a tree . . .
EUREKA!
Squad! It's time to go! Now!

# CHAPTER 3: ALL'S FAIR AT THE SUPER-SCIENCE FAIR

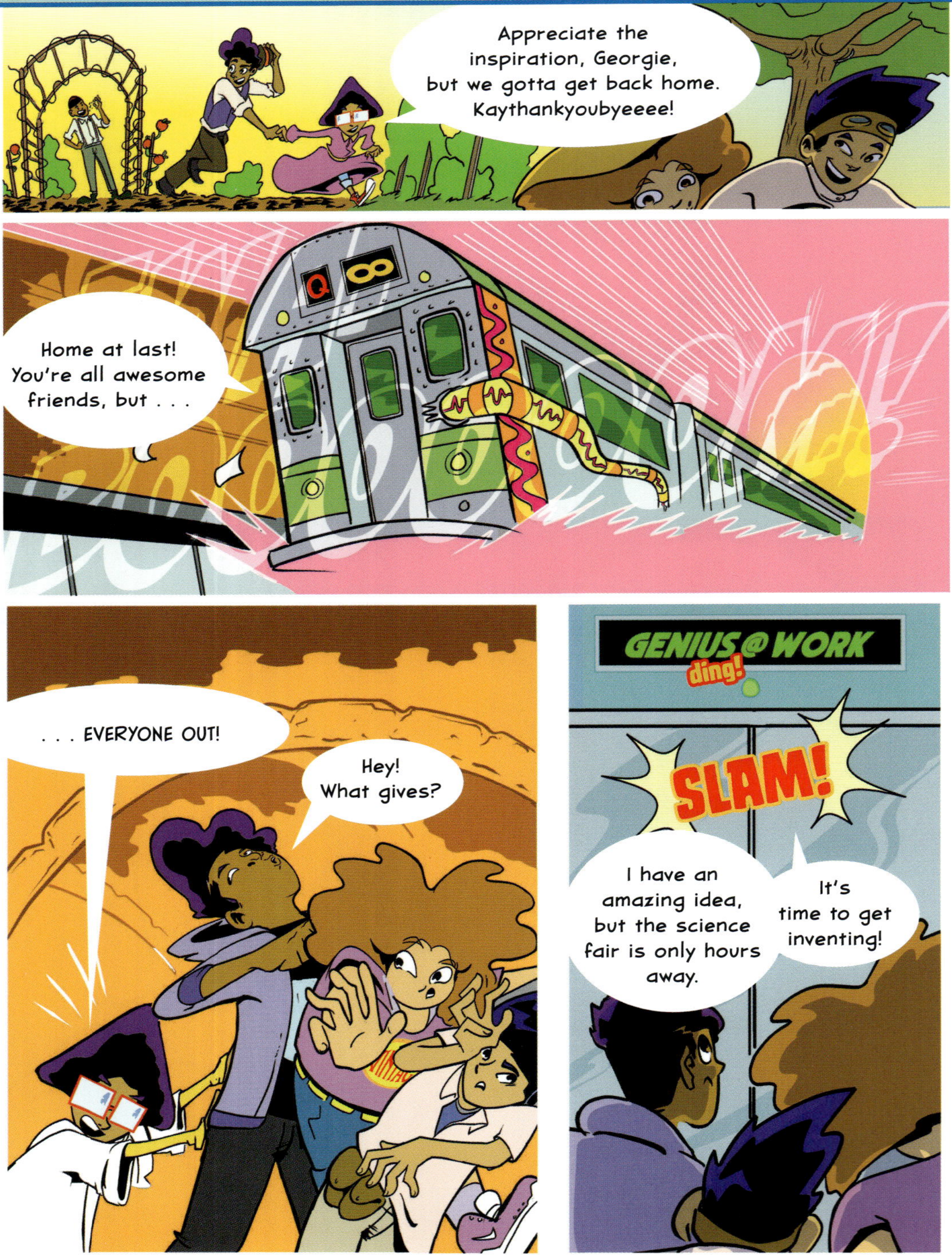
Appreciate the inspiration, Georgie, but we gotta get back home. Kaythankyoubyeeee!
Q
Home at last! You're all awesome friends, but . . .
. . . EVERYONE OUT!
Hey! What gives?
GENIUS@WORK
ding!
SLAM!
I have an amazing idea, but the science fair is only hours away.
It's time to get inventing!

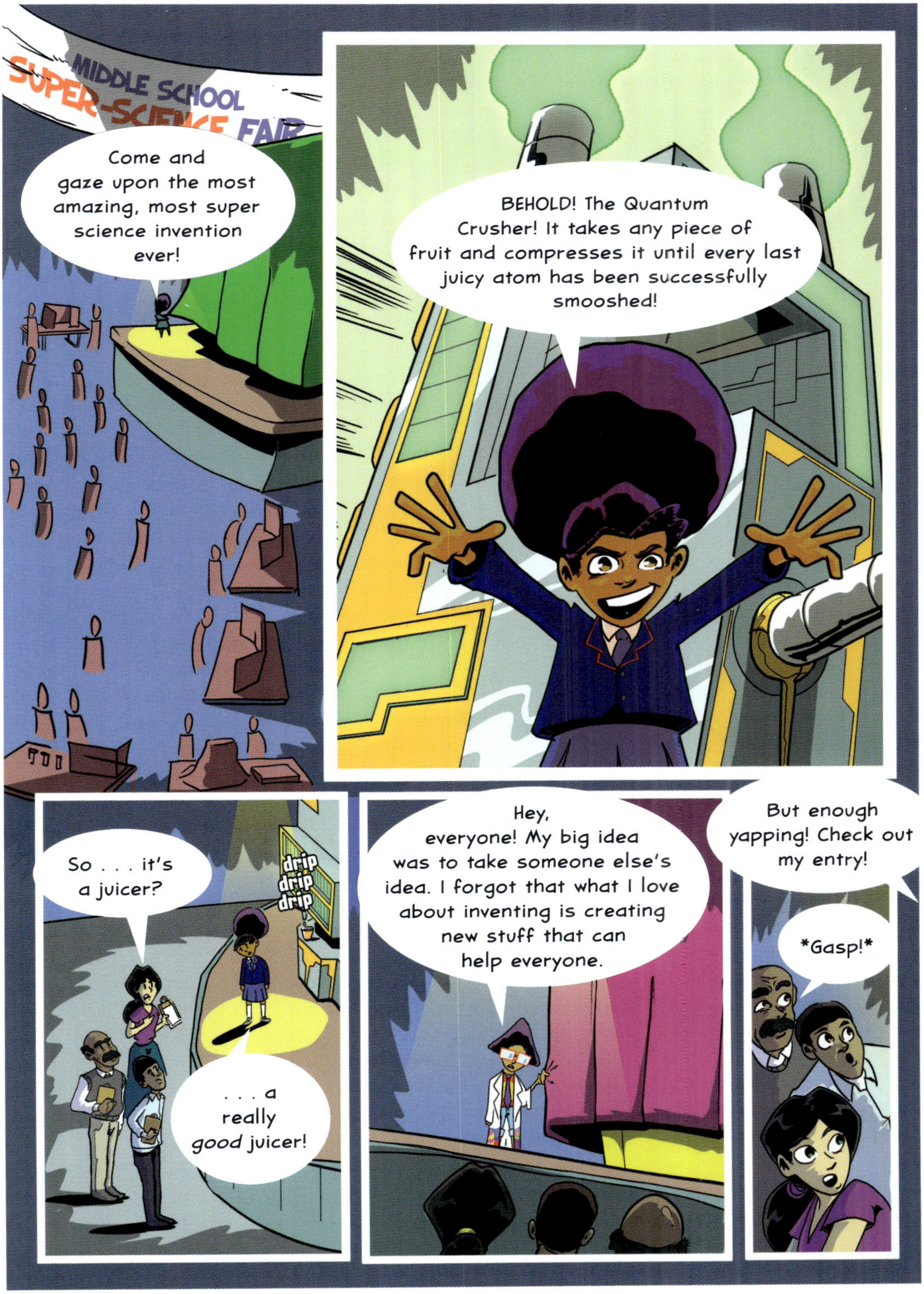
MIDDLE SCHOOL
SUPER-SCIENCE FAIR
Come and gaze upon the most amazing, most super science invention ever!
BEHOLD! The Quantum Crusher! It takes any piece of fruit and compresses it until every last juicy atom has been successfully smooshed!
So . . . it's a juicer?
drip drip drip
. . . a really *good* juicer!
Hey, everyone! My big idea was to take someone else's idea. I forgot that what I love about inventing is creating new stuff that can help everyone.
But enough yapping! Check out my entry!
*Gasp!*

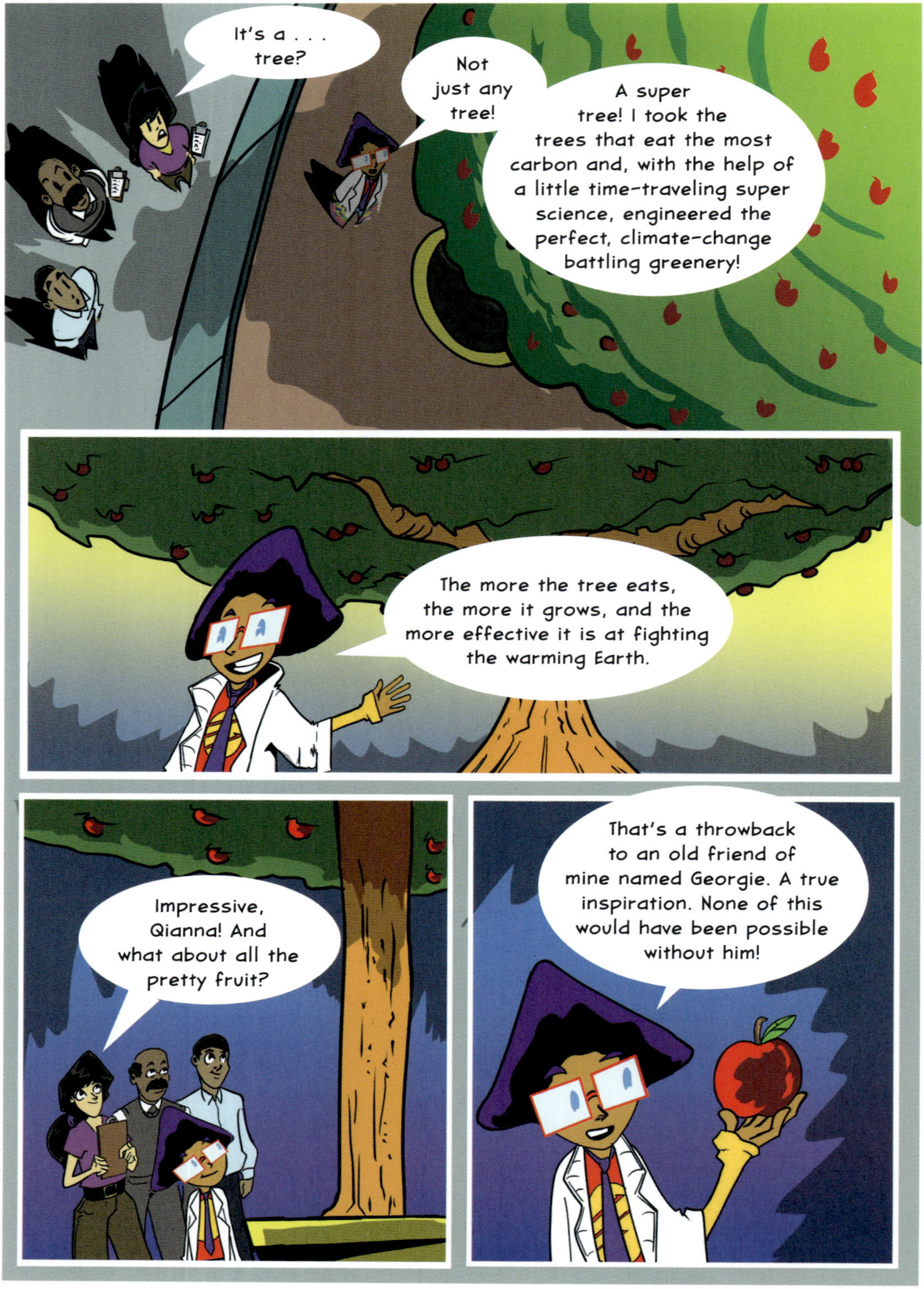
It's a . . . tree?
Not just any tree!
A super tree! I took the trees that eat the most carbon and, with the help of a little time-traveling super science, engineered the perfect, climate-change battling greenery!
The more the tree eats, the more it grows, and the more effective it is at fighting the warming Earth.
Impressive, Qianna! And what about all the pretty fruit?
That's a throwback to an old friend of mine named Georgie. A true inspiration. None of this would have been possible without him!

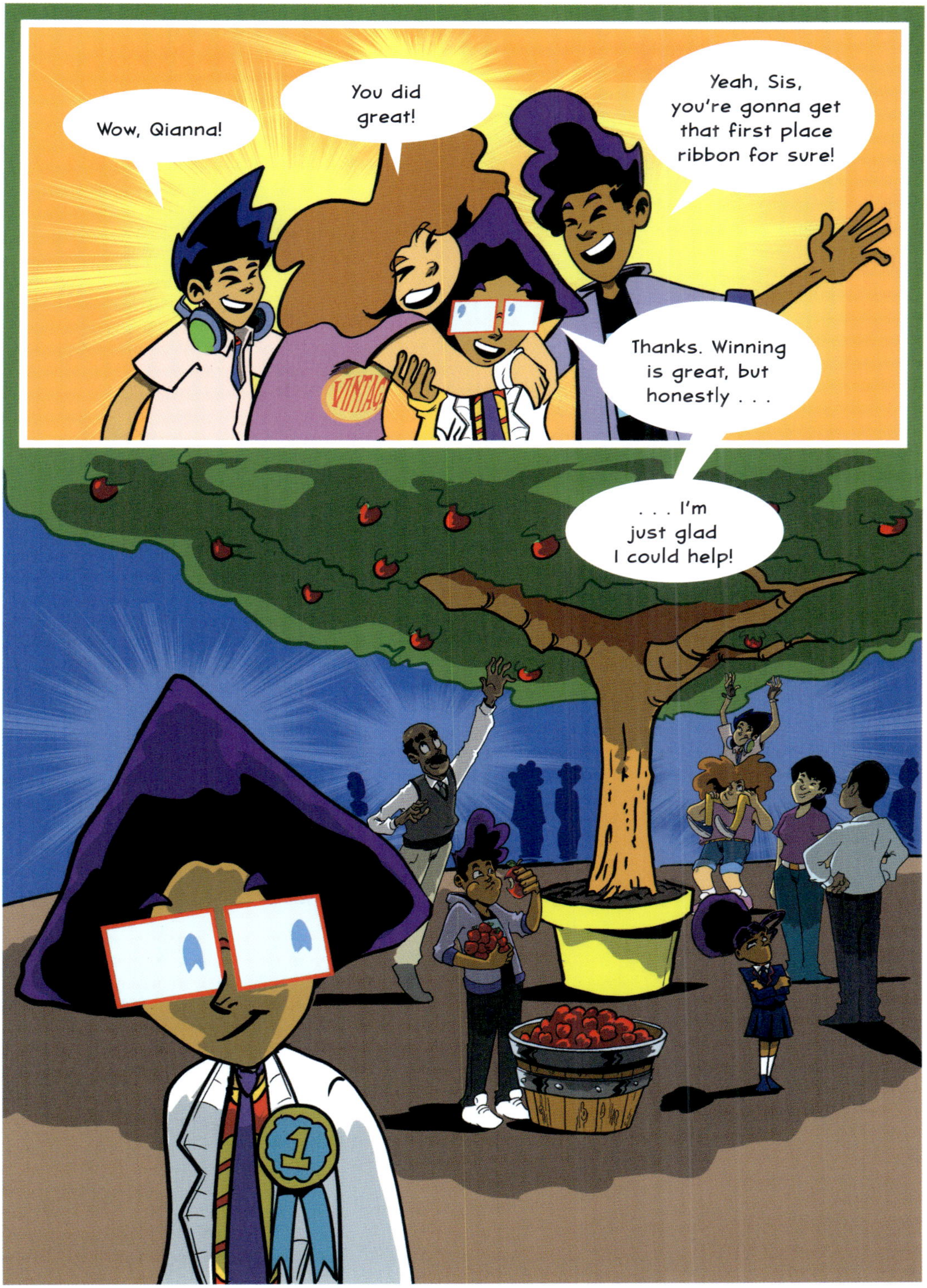
Wow, Qianna!
You did great!
Yeah, Sis, you're gonna get that first place ribbon for sure!
Thanks. Winning is great, but honestly . . .
. . . I'm just glad I could help!
VINTAG

# HOW TO FILE A PATENT

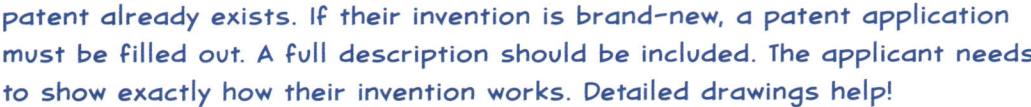

United States Patent and Trademark Office

Patents give inventors ownership over their creation. They keep other people from making or selling that invention for their own financial gain. Patents must be filed with the government. Sometimes, a fee must be paid.

Anyone interested in filing a patent must follow some instructions. First, they need to see if the patent already exists. If their invention is brand-new, a patent application must be filled out. A full description should be included. The applicant needs to show exactly how their invention works. Detailed drawings help!

Once the application is filed, it is reviewed by the patent office. They may ask for additional information. If the application meets all the requirements, a patent is granted. More fees might need to be paid.

Patents don't last forever. Maintenance fees must be paid every few years to keep the patent. After twenty years, the patent term ends. After this, other people can use and build their own versions of the invention.

Provisional Application for Patent
Personal Information

1 Fill out a patent application.

ED STATES PATENT SHEET 10
11
17
8

2 Provide details of how the invention works.

3 If requirements are met, the patent is granted.

# TIME TUTOR SHOUT-OUT!

## FACTS ABOUT GEORGE WASHINGTON CARVER
### 1864–1943

George Washington Carver was born enslaved in 1864 or 1865. He was freed shortly after the Civil War (1861–1865) ended.

Young Carver had an early appreciation for nature and learning. He liked to take walks and observe what he saw.

The George Washington Carver National Monument was dedicated in 1943. It is Carver's childhood home in Missouri. The monument was the first one named for a Black American.

Carver earned a master's degree in agricultural science from Iowa State University. He taught at Tuskegee University for forty-seven years.

# GLOSSARY

**black hole** (BLAK HOLE)—an invisible region of space with a strong gravitational field

**chemurgy** (KEM-ur-jee)—a branch of chemistry that turns farm products into industrial products

**chronal** (KROW-nuhl)—relating to time

**engineering** (en-juh-NEER-ing)—the application of science to practical use

**global warming** (GLOW-buhl WARM-ing)—the rise in the average worldwide temperature of the troposphere

**heist** (HIEST)—an armed robbery

**integrity** (in-TEG-ruh-tee)—total honesty and sincerity

**invention** (in-VEN-shuhn)—a new idea

**malady** (MAL-uh-dee)—a disease or ailment

**patent** (PAT-uhnt)—the right to be the only one to make, use, or sell an invention for a certain number of years

**quantum** (KWAN-tuhm)—a unit of energy

**ronin** (ROE-nihn)—a samurai who had left his master or whose master had died

**singularity** (sing-yoo-LARE-uh-tee)—a hypothetical future point in time

# READ MORE

Loh-Hagan, Virginia. *Excellence in STEM*. Ann Arbor, MI: Cherry Lake Publishing, 2022.

Miller, J. P. *Groundbreaking Scientists*. New York: Crabtree Publishing Company, 2021.

Parkin, Michelle. *George Washington Carver*. Chicago: Norwood House Press, 2023.

# INTERNET SITES

*Britannica Kids: George Washington Carver*
kids.britannica.com/kids/article/George-Washington-Carver/352918

*Kiddle: Patent Facts for Kids*
kids.kiddle.co/Patent

*National Geographic Kids: George Washington Carver*
kids.nationalgeographic.com/history/article/george-washington-carver

## ABOUT THE AUTHOR/ILLUSTRATOR

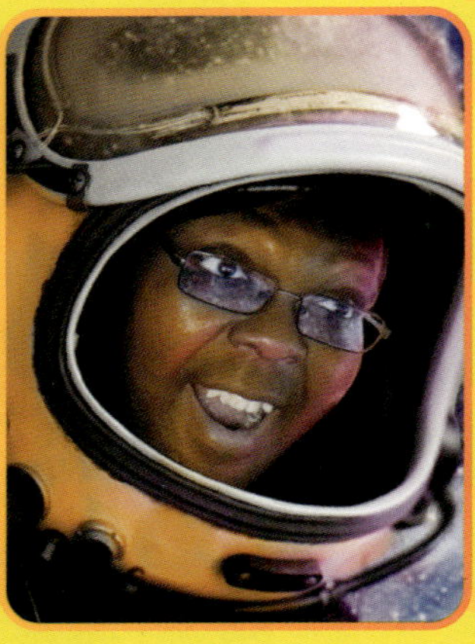

Jared Sams is a writer, producer, and self-taught artist. He channels his hip-hop and punk music influences to imbue his work with all the weirdness and imagination that he can muster. Jared strives to create impactful stories that promote empathy and advocate for the voiceless.

## BOOKS IN THIS SERIES

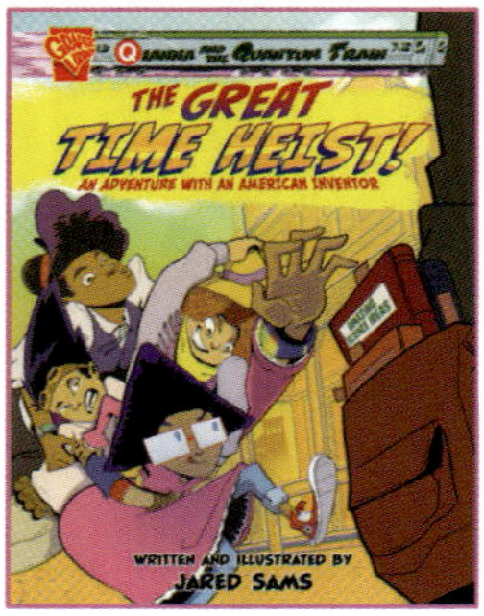
THE GREAT TIME HEIST!
AN ADVENTURE WITH AN AMERICAN INVENTOR
WRITTEN AND ILLUSTRATED BY
JARED SAMS

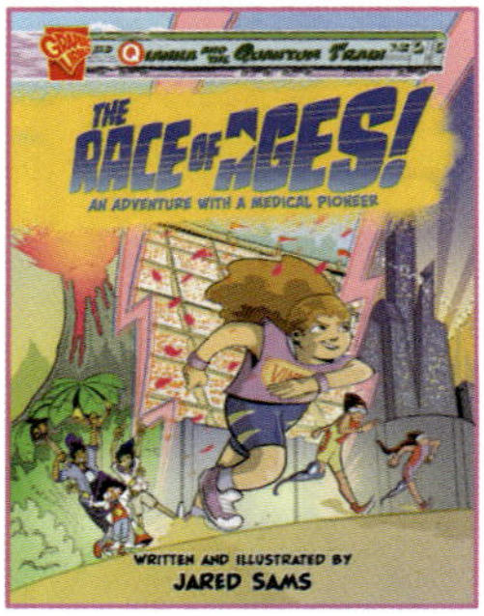
THE RACE OF AGES!
AN ADVENTURE WITH A MEDICAL PIONEER
WRITTEN AND ILLUSTRATED BY
JARED SAMS

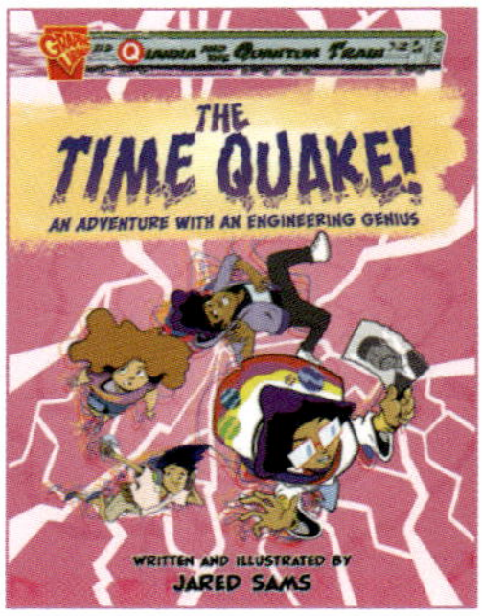
THE TIME QUAKE!
AN ADVENTURE WITH AN ENGINEERING GENIUS
WRITTEN AND ILLUSTRATED BY
JARED SAMS

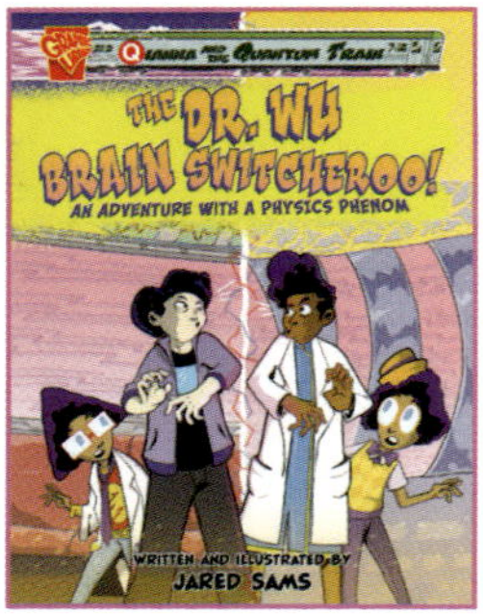
THE DR. WU BRAIN SWITCHEROO!
AN ADVENTURE WITH A PHYSICS PHENOM
WRITTEN AND ILLUSTRATED BY
JARED SAMS